The Shapes of Our Screams

T T Madden

SLASHIC HORROR PRESS

Praise for Shapes of Our Screams

"In *The Shapes of Our Screams,* music is a living, breathing cosmic power, a force for self-discovery and connection. It's also a force for unfathomable destruction. Madden's skill shines in this exploration of identity and belonging set against a backdrop of terrifying fascist carnage. I loved this timely story."

J.A.W. McCarthy, Bram Stoker Award and Shirley Jackson Award finalist, author of Sleep Alone

"A slick and deep nightmare into America's greatest legacies, its love of music and violence."

Rachel Bolton, Stoker Award-nominee of She Had Been So Reasonable

"Darrow Foroi is a band on the road, working and wanting to make a mark for themselves, but the tour is merely a catalyst for their journey. The real stuff is in their navigating the social, political, and emotional landscape around them, coming to grips with horrors both terrifyingly real and surreal.

The prose is simple, clean, effective, and oh, so addictive. Echoes the pragmatic beauty of Hemingway with subtle, lovely notes of Faulkner. It expresses the fear, rage, and heartbreak of what it's like to be queer in MAGA America. Getting to know Lo taught me a little about what it's like to be a fluid, queer person. I am grateful for the look inside.

The horror takes its time and creeps in subtly, in Stephen King-esque fashion. And what a horror: alien, supernatural, and all-too-eerily familiar as it is relevant.

That is the true horror here."

Mark Justice, author of Death's Head: The Eye of Samedi

GUEST PARKING FIELD
COSTUMING
OFFICES
FENCE
VENDOR STALLS
KILN
ENTRANCE
FOOD & TAVERN
VENDOR STALLS
SOUTH STAGE
FENCE
N
W
E
S

RV PARKING
NORTH STAGE
STOCKS
GRAND STAGE
CHAPEL
JOUSTING PIT
Questing Beast
RENAISSANCE FESTIVAL

For everyone who's ever been told they're too loud.

Be louder.

DARROW FOR OI
TRACK·LIST
Side A
I: Worm
II: The River
III: Cult of the White Flame
IV: The Spear
Side B
V: The Demagogue
VI: The Festival of the Fallen Moon
VII: Tithes
VIII: Stand Before a God
IX: Godkiller
X: The Holes in the Worlds
FUCK.
HATE.

SIDE A

Holstenwall Prison holds only one inmate; Worm. The walls are all they've known, all they've ever seen, sustenance tossed down from a hole in the ceiling, their only sight of the sky. Sometimes they think the prison grew up around them the moment they were born.

– From Darrow Foroi's liner notes

2023

Lo TENSES AS THE car finally crosses the state line from Georgia into Florida. Micah, seeing their reaction as they cross the border, reaches over from the driver's seat and takes their hand. Squeezes tight.

"It'll be alright," he says. He's said it before, and Lo knows he'll say it again before showtime. Before the day's out. Hell, probably before they even reach the motel. Nevertheless, Lo squeezes back, their pale hand in his dark one, and believes him. Or at least tells themself to.

Micah's never let you down before.

The dysphoria hits Lo hard, and they pull one leg over the other, suddenly extremely self-conscious of how they're dressed, how they've styled their hair, every single thing about the cage of their corporeality. A padded bra pushes up their tank top emblazoned with the band's name, Darrow Foroi, and logo; that crackling, thorny heavy metal text with a sword slicing vertically through it. The shirt exposes their arms, skin decorated with various tattoos; a broadsword with a broken blade on their right forearm, a centipede winding around it, a cracked egg below their collarbone, a large moth with a beautiful face in its wings on their left shoulder. The long and arduous process of waxing their body is worth it whenever they look down and feel like they are finally looking at *their* legs, not someone else's hairy appendages that just happen to be attached to them. Smooth, hairless legs with feet planted in Toms. Legs sheathed in short shorts with just enough looseness in the front to conceal the slight bulge of Lo's genitals. Their head full of tight curls is only waiting to explode in the Florida humidity, but for now they're shorter in the back and sides, parted so that they bunch over the left side of Lo's face, partially covering their eye. Lo checks in the sun visor mirror and sees their makeup is still in place; dark lipstick and eyeshadow, just like any self-respecting rock singer. A little bit of extra help that makes them feel like *them* and not like *him*.

The whole look is very fluid, helps Lo achieve their desired appearance goal; androgyny. They spend a long time working towards such a goal, but they're still unable to entirely articulate why it's so important to them that people not know entirely who or what they are. They've filled multiple notebooks with attempts to explain those feelings—in song or otherwise—but Lo still hasn't really gotten it down yet. Those emotions only ever come out as harsh scratches they can only imagine screaming into a microphone.

Fashion has changed a lot recently. Lo dressing like they do, wearing makeup, a padded bra, generally isn't considered weird anymore. But that's in places farther north. People rarely gave Lo weird looks in Philadelphia, in D.C., in Baltimore. There are other people like them in those places. But they are in a much different place now.

Lo watches as the Georgia license plates around them slowly disappear, replaced with Florida ones, and they let go of Micah's hand, aware and self-conscious of the amount of sweat gathering between their palms.

What they have come here to do is illegal.

The people in charge here would like to make Lo's very existence illegal.

A few weeks ago, Darrow Foroi was offered a chance to play a live show at a venue in Florida. A concert along with several other bands after hours at a local renaissance festival. The catch? It was secret show, because all the bands would be, technically speaking, illegal under the state's new anti-drag laws. The guy hosting the show was giving all the money from tickets to LGBT+ youth in Florida. The secret had already gotten out to a degree; there'd been whispers of it online, money slipped to a queer-friendly security guard, vendors "accidentally" leaving access to power cables, potential fairgoers preparing for the event in the same way they'd prepare for a protest; bringing masks, covering tattoos, leaving phones at home. The secrecy and the danger made Lo think about the Underground Railroad, which at first seemed like an absurd comparison to them. Or was it? Or would it be in a few years?

A long and very serious conversation occurred when Micah told the band about the offer. A conversation that took all night even though the decision itself took only moments. Even though none of the other band members were anything other than cis het men, they all told Lo they'd wear dresses right alongside them. Solidarity. Rebellion. Punk. That's the whole reason they started such a band in the first place. Putting their records on the line. Their livelihoods.

Maybe even their actual lives.

Despite the risks, they decided to go. To the state the NAACP advised Micah not to. Deep into the heart of the state that could—and would, if they were seen—arrest them all and label them child predators simply because of the way they planned on dressing. The place that wanted to give them the death penalty. Legally or otherwise.

They knew they had to go. Aware that there's a special kind of horror to the terrible things that happen in the daylight. Lo wonders if all the people throughout time who called themselves rebels felt as scared as they do now.

The walkie-talkie on the dashboard squawks and Lo hears Evan's voice: "We're here, we're queer!" In the background, Danny and Tijo whoop and holler. Again, Lo is glad they rode with Micah. They don't know if they could handle that level of *up* on top of all the stress they already feel.

Micah snatches the walkie off the dash, looks into the rear-view mirror as he says, in his Serious Voice, "Quit fuckin' around back there."

Lo looks over their shoulder and sees the black band van behind them, the one that a moment ago had been edging closer to the median strip and our bumper like the boys were trying to shoot into our backseat, suddenly straighten out.

Micah, their guitarist, is more the band dad than he is the leader (there really is no leader). He's always given off a big Hendrix vibe, even before they started Darrow Foroi; the same goatee, funky shirts in wild colors, vests. His hair, however, is more Marley, shoulder-length locks that usually stay pulled back behind his head unless they're playing. The only one of them who isn't covered in tattoos, Micah only has, technically, one; a sleeve on his right arm depicting various figures of the Harlem Renaissance. Every year for Christmas Micah would get a new book from a different Black writer, someone he'd never even heard about in his public school. He said his parents always wanted him to learn more than what people wanted him to know. That was part of the reason why he became a public school teacher, and why he decided to do it in Baltimore.

From the walkie, Evan says, "Yes, Dad", and Lo sees him give a choppy salute from the passenger's seat. Evan is their drummer, covered head-to-toe in tattoos. If he'd shaved his mop of hair he'd look like a skinhead, which tracked, since he'd managed to extricate himself from a family of them before he, too, became brainwashed. When he isn't drumming, he's usually tattooing, covering up fascist tattoos for free. A skater in middle school who never outgrew the style, the Florida heat is much easier on him and his basketball shorts and tank top. He'll fit in well with the beach bums.

Micah squawks back, "We don't want to get arrested before we even get there."

Yeah, Lo thinks, *that would make our arrest when we finally do get there essentially meaningless.* They aren't sure who's really at risk among the various members of Darrow Foroi, but Lo knows for sure they are the one at the top of the pyramid, their WANTED poster higher and larger than anyone else's. Fitting, they guess, for a lead singer. They think of the imaginary crimes that would decorate it, and try to feel like a rebel instead of just a scared child.

THE BAND PULLS INTO the parking lot of a MacReady's superstore, their final pit stop before their journey is complete. The motel is another ninety minutes away according to Micah, but the boys in the van with all the gear just can't hang on.

They gotta pee.

They're hungry.

They're thirsty.

They needle the team dad until he agrees to pull over at the next big-box-style store to fill up on fuel for the cars and themselves.

Everyone piles haphazardly out of both vehicles, an avalanche of perceived deviancy spilling into the Florida sun.

Danny, their bass player, looks like he's going to faint the moment he steps outside. His natural habitat is much closer to their end goal of the tree-canopy-covered renaissance festival than out in the brutal sun; a six-and-a-half foot tall bear with a bushy beard and equally long hair. He'd made it out of this environment before, going from construction worker to foreman, and it looks like a return to that heat is doing him few favors. The bucket hat atop his head is doing very little to cool him down, and the small personal fan even less.

Tijo, their keyboardist, has been mistaken for a Latin gang member more than once, with his bald head and copious tattoos. People look at him with bugged-out eyes or give him a wide berth when they're coming down the street.

They have no idea he comes from a rich family, the kind of people who paid for a private piano tutor multiple times a week when he was in grade school. And yet none of that seems to matter because of what he looks like now. Tijo always smiles and shakes it off, says it at least gave him enough material to write their song "The River", one of their biggest hits.

But Lo can tell peoples' perception of Tijo bothers him in the same way Lo is bothered when someone calls them *dude* or *guy* or *sir*. A skin-crawling sensation that's difficult to entirely articulate.

And finally there's Lo, lead vocals. Lo for the band, but Lorenzo on their driver's license. Though Micah's never said it aloud, Lo suspects that's part of the reason he always offers to drive. Just in case they get pulled over.

All together, they are Darrow Foroi. They call themselves a rock band to keep it short and simple, even though they know they have plenty of genre mashup. Within them, there are bits of prog-rock and classical, a dash of hip-hop whenever Micah's vocals kick in. Someone once compared them to Linkin Park (in the Chester era, of course), which every one of them took as an enormous compliment. They all wanted to be recognizable, comparable, but still be their own thing, and, for each member of the band, what sets them apart from everyone else, why their hearts are really in it, is the world they've created together.

Darrow Foroi's music is wrapped in a narrative, a concept album that builds out a fictional mythology of the kind one review graciously compared to what Coheed and Cambria has done. The album tells the story of a character known as Worm, who escapes from confinement in an abandoned prison and travels around a dangerous, dark fantasy world called Alor (pronounced like *allure*). The band's name, Darrow Foroi, comes from a mythological place within the world of Alor, a Valhalla-type paradise Worm is seeking.

And now, like Worm, they've arrived in a place that is actively hostile to them.

Or at least that's how it seems. Lo has no idea what the state of Florida is *actually* like—this is their first time here—but if it's anything like how the news makes it out to be, the locals must be horrified at what has just come spilling out into their world.

The reality seems different, though. A couple of people give them looks, sure, but by and large they're only clocked as existing, paid attention to only as other bodies to avoid so shoppers can get to where they need to go. Nothing personal. Lo doesn't see any threats, but they flinch when they hear a distant popping sound. A moment later they realize it's just a truck backfiring.

Maybe it's not like what they say it is, Lo thinks, and feels some stress leak out of their shoulders and upper back as all around them the boys stretch out the kinks from the long ride. Danny wipes sweat from under his bucket hat. Tijo cracks his back. Evan stretches his legs. Micah tells them fifteen minutes, tops, that they need to get back on the road.

Maybe everything will be okay.

"You alright, girl?"

Lo looks around, finds Evan looking at them, his eyebrows raised. The rest of the guys know how Lo feels about gendered greetings, to stay away from the male ones entirely. They developed a running gag of using the most ostentatious ones possible—your *buckaroos* or *hooligans*—after a show a couple years ago when Danny struggled to address Lo. He'd wanted to be inclusive, tried his best to find a good word for the whole room, but the gears in his brain wouldn't click together even when *everyone* was right there. He'd settled on *compatriots*, like he was a general giving a wartime speech, even lifting a hand to emphasize the word. The whole room, Danny included, exploded with laughter. But those greetings were meant for goofing off. Lo can tell by the look in Evan's eyes he's being serious.

"I'm alright," Lo says, nevertheless looking out over the parking lot again. They think they hear that distant popping yet again, like fireworks somewhere they can't see. Is it really a truck? "I'm gonna hang out here while y'all go in, I think."

"You sure?" Evan asks.

Lo nods.

"You want me to stay with you?"

"Nah." Lo shakes their head, curls bouncing. They can already feel the humidity working its way in to their hair. "I can entertain myself."

Evan continues to look at them for another moment, as if to triple-check if they're sure, and Lo is both touched and mildly annoyed at what seems like coddling, but what they know is really genuine care. They remind themself that two seemingly contradictory things can be felt together. They wish it wasn't true, that feelings were much easier to feel, but that's reality. They can be both grateful for Evan, and want him to treat them like an adult.

After a moment, Evan says, "Cool, you want anything?"

Lo is about to say, "Nothing" before a cloud moves out of the way and the Florida sun starts burning itself into the back of their exposed neck.

"Soda," they say, moving into the shade next to the van.

"Roger dodger," Evan nods and follows the guys in the direction of the store.

Lo leans against the side of the van, in what little shadow they can get, looks around the parking lot and sees an enormous pickup truck approaching them through the rows of cars. It's an immaculate white and flies, paradoxically, both American and Confederate flags out of its bed. The huge, obnoxious vehicle barrels through the parking lot much faster than the other cars, screeches its way towards and then past Lo, careening into two opens spots near the front of the store.

Lo sees Don't Tread On Me bumper stickers and machine gun and Second Amendment decals spread out across the back of the truck, a giant MAGA decal across the back window, and they keep to the shadow of the van. Their heart pounds and their shoulders tense. They don't think what they're wearing now constitutes "drag", except for the bra, but they don't want to take that chance.

Not here.

Not alone.

So they very slowly get back into Micah's car, sink low into the seat, watch the vehicle and its driver in the mirrors. They hear the big engine rumble to a stop, the truck coming to a rest like a sleeping dragon. Through the mirrors they see a man hop down to the concrete, adjust his baseball cap and the pistol tucked into the back of his jeans. He saunters away from the truck and towards the store, and after a moment of complete and rational fear, Lo realizes this is just the way of some people in this part of the country. That the man has a gun, but doesn't intend to go into the store and use it. They are in a part of the country where people just walk around with them, like a shiny, lethal appendage. Phone, keys, wallet, gun.

Lo realizes all that; this man is not a direct threat to them. They tell themself they've faced similar anxieties, that their aftermath always happens the same way. They know exactly how it'll go because this is how it's gone before with other men, other dangers; Lo will be unable to stay still for awhile, unable to rest, unable to sleep, their thoughts filled with the presence of that danger, even though it will not be there anymore. Days will go by, and they will think of it less and less, but it will still be a recurring fear, a boogeyman that pops up every once-in-a-while to remind them there are still dangers in the world, and there are even more for a person like them.

THERE IS THAT OLD question: if a tree falls in the forest and no one is around to hear it, does it make a sound? Hard to say about trees, but all kinds of sounds have been recorded without the presence of man, such as the mysterious, underwater Bloop or the Ping.

But not this one.

This is a sound unlike anything that's ever been recorded before, let alone heard by human ears. If it were to be heard, it might at first be described as a truck backfiring, or firecrackers. Maybe even the rapid-fire pull of a semi-automatic trigger, its beat increasing and decreasing without a clear pattern. Something quantifiable and explainable in terms of the experiences of a human being. *Pop…pop pop-pop-pop…pop…pop.* Bouncing off the sky. Echoing off the trees and leaves, the moss and water of the Florida swamp. This sound has been other places before, has moved across space and time, through other spaces and other times, traveling unquantifiable routes, but this is where it has found itself now. Deep in the swamp. Surrounded by trees, by water. Moss and algae. No human ears within miles to hear it.

After a while a pattern coalesces out of that chaos, and the beats become rhythmic.

It becomes something else.

It is music.

Legends say the Divis River was carved by a single soldier, a half-mile-wide cleft gouged into the world as if by magic. Standing on the riverbank, Worm wonders who would go through so much effort, do so much work, all to isolate their own country.

– From Darrow Foroi's liner notes

Lo isn't used to the flatness of the Florida landscape. Things were bigger in their hometown of Beacon, Ohio, much farther north than here, in the middle of the country with mountains, rivers, and lakes. Where *open* is instead the operative word. Open, and yet still not empty. Lo thinks it's *too* open down here, like something could come at them from the sky as well as the ground. They try to push that thought away, tell themselves nothing is going to happen; they're with the band. The boys won't let anything happen to them.

But it might not be up to them, a sneering little voice in the back of Lo's head tells them.

The Palm Grove Motel sits under an open sky that's touched only by its namesake trees. Lo can see a couple of iguanas in those trees, just hanging there like scaly squirrels. They know already that Evan will be fascinated with the animals, hopes he won't be foolish enough to try and catch one. If he does, Micah will put a stop to it.

Micah pulls them into a parking spot in front of their room, 42, and Tijo pulls the van in next to them. Their corner of the building is backed up against swampland, which Lo imagines they can probably see through a window in the bathroom, and there's another entrance on the side.

They realize they're looking for exits again, planning for the inevitability of disaster.

"You wanna stay here?" Micah asks, and Lo again feels that bubble of anger like they're being coddled. This unreasonable feeling, mixed as it is with affection.

It's because they care for you. They say, "No, I'll come with you."

Micah looks surprised, but says nothing to discourage it, and together they walk into the office while the rest of the boys stretch and unload. Micah does all the talking as he normally does, the perks of being with someone who's somehow even *more* type-A than Lo.

While Micah talks, Lo watches the man behind the counter, just as he watches them. He's tall, older, bits of gray sprinkled in his hair, and thick-framed glasses, a simple polo shirt. He engages with Micah, answers all his questions, but they come slower than Lo guesses they would were they not there. He's distracted, looking from Micah to Lo, looking Lo up and down, and they know exactly what's going on in his head. The questions, wondering how to categorize them. Other people might assume he was perving, some sexual parasite, but Lo knew better. They'd experienced that gaze too many times, the eyes that said, *What the fuck is that?* Eyes that attempted to categorize them.

Lo fights the urge to step to their left, to hide ever-so-slightly behind Micah, to give in to the look, to let the man's eyes overpower them. For a second, they think about going back to the way they used to be, to the *he* they used to be, but it's not possible to put that Humpty Dumpty back together. They know the confused and curious stares are going to be like this at the show, are going to be like this everywhere they go, and they know they have to fight through it.

Because they can't go back. Not ever.

Not to that cage.

"Alright," the man says, sliding a sleeve of plastic motel room cards across the counter to Micah. "Hope you and your...girlfriend have a nice stay at the Palm Grove Motel." The man sounds like he struggles with the word. It's with the specific inflection that Lo can guess his type—the kind who doesn't get it, but decides it isn't worth the trouble. He'll probably only ever see Lo and Micah one more time in his entire life—at checkout. Nevertheless, it causes a swell in Lo's chest, one big enough to drown out the awkward thought of intimacy with Micah.

"Thanks, pal." Micah swipes the keys and gives Lo a look as they head out into the parking lot. As they approach the boys, he says, "The guy hopes me and my *girlfriend* have a nice time."

The boys erupt into a chorus of jeers and *ooh*s. Danny smiles wide, pumps his eyebrows up at them suggestively. Tijo makes kissing noises in their direction. Evan does something Lo thinks no one has done since the actual 1990s; he turns around, wraps his arms around himself and undulates in place, the illusion of making out with someone.

But instead of making them blush, the jeers only egg Lo on, and before they realize it, they're smiling, playing right along. They know the reactions are overdone for their sake, to emphasise just how much they all love Lo, and it makes their heart sing.

"Please," they say, giving the boys a quick pirouette. "Y'all wish you could get some of this." It's an uncharacteristic move, this sudden confidence, but they're buoyed by their bandmates.

The jeers turn to whoops of approval and they all start moving, jumping and bobbing to their own individual soundtracks. Completely out of sync and bumping into one another, it doesn't matter as their own musics fill them. Evan starts spitting some ska-adjacent beat, Tijo dancing erratically to it, Danny doing the classic low-effort bob from one foot to the next, back again, shoulders swaying. Micah whips his dreads and Lo jumps into the middle of all of them, moving their hips in an explicitly feminine way. Their musics flow through them until laughter consumes them, and their energy fast burns out, sapped by the Florida sun. Lo realizes they're sweating, and their makeup's probably running, and their hair is exploding in the humidity, but the boys don't notice. They don't care, and neither does Lo. They're all together and everything's okay.

THEY HAVE TWO MOTEL rooms, connected to one another by adjoining doors. Evan, Tijo, and Danny are in one, Lo and Micah in the other. They don't bother to take anything other than their overnight bags out of the cars. Before they're unpacked, Micah picks blades of grass from the lawn and they draw straws to see who will go get the night's pizza. Evan doesn't look too mad about it when he loses, but before he leaves, Micah stops them all while they're together.

"Everyone's gotta be up at seven tomorrow, okay?" He reminds the group even though he's already done so ten thousand times—and no doubt will ten thousand more. They're supposed to head to the faire in the morning and meet the owner, have him show them around. The band all gives Micah various answers in the affirmative, and he in turn reminds them all of his commitment to blasting calypso music into the ears of anyone who isn't awake on time.

When Evan heads out, Lo goes into the bathroom to take off their makeup and wash themself of some of the day's sweat. In peeling off their top and padded bra, they realize they need a full shower instead, even if it's just a rinse, and turn the cold water faucet. Just being in the same room as the cold pressure blast is enough to fight away the oppressive Florida heat. As Lo strips, they try to avoid looking in the mirror. They tell themself not to, but it's like the call of the void, all too darkly tempting, and once they're nude they open one eye, then the other.

Naked in the mirror, Lo is unmistakable as what they are not. The tucking and slimming gone from their silhouette, the attempt at an hourglass ripped away, they're faced with their natural Burke shape, the cock dangling between their legs. They try to steer into the skid, make a couple muscles in the mirror, think maybe they can convince themself tonight they belong more towards the masc end of the spectrum, but it doesn't work. They knew it wouldn't as soon as they saw their reflection.

Lo jumps away from the mirror and into the cold shower. Goosebumps prickle their skin and the cold shrinks their dick, makes their balls crawl up for warmth, and that retreat makes them feel a little bit more like themself.

Whenever they're naked, faced with the reality of their physicality, it's much harder to feel how they really feel. That's part of why sex has taken somewhat of a backseat since Lo's started exploring gender within the last few years. They don't really know what to do when their largest erogenous zone is a part of them they often want to be rid of. They're sure someone out there knows how to make it work, that someone just isn't them. At least not yet.

There was one time, one guy, directly after a show, where things had begun to feel a little more right. Lo felt more like themself than they ever had before, fresh after a set, the crowd screaming all around them, everyone partying in the aftermath. They found themself in the green room with one of those adoring fans, a big man with sleeve tattoos, their lips on his, their hands at his waist. Lo's head swam, not entirely sure what role they wanted to take in this until he grabbed them by their upper arms and pushed them against the wall.

Oh.

Yes.

There it was.

Like a switch was flipped in their head, lighting up a neon sign that said *femme*. When the guy reached around behind Lo and grabbed their ass with both hands, Lo pushed off the wall, helped him boost them up against it. Their legs spread and wrapped around his waist, held him tight like there was a chance he could blow away as he carried them over to the couch.

Against the velvet fabric, Lo's hands snaked down to his belt, ripped open his fly and dove into his underwear, through his nest of pubic hair, his cock in their hand, warm and hard and dripping with excitement. Together, they furiously pulled at the ruffles of Lo's skirt to get it up and away. Why did they have to wear something so goddamn long and ruffly? Their breath was hot in one another's mouths, and when Lo whispered, "Fuck me," when they turned around to offer themself from behind, the man whispered something in response. Something so low Lo almost didn't hear it.

Lo hitched. Like they hit a record scratch.

"What did you say?" There was still a bit of that breathy edge in their voice, but it was already wilting. They knew what he said, were already replaying it.

"Nothing," the guy said, even though he still dug at their skirt, grabbed at their hair, still pushed his face into Lo's neck, teeth still nipping, cock rubbing against their ass. He had them pressed against the back of the couch, and there was nowhere for them to go, so they pushed back against him. Ass pressed against his pelvis, pushing his cock into his belly. They whirled around and looked him in the face.

I've never been with a trans girl before. That's what he said.

Lo asked, "What do you think this is?"

"What do you mean?" he replied, still trying to come closer. Pulling at them. But Lo didn't let him.

"Do you think this is some kind of trophy hunt?"

He chuckled his way through a "What? No." But those words, that expression, were a lie. They knew what he really wanted. An experiment. An exploration. Something to conquer. Lo wondered how much trans porn they'd find on his phone if they looked.

"No, no, we're not doing this." Lo pushed him away, and he stumbled back with his pants drooping around his hips.

"What the fuck?" His voice raised a little too high, too aggressive. Even though Lo had at that point never had the lived experience of denying a man to his face a body he thinks he is owed, they knew enough for an alarm bell to signal at his raised voice.

"You're just gonna fucking leave me like this?" He gestured down to his dick, still hard, poking out of his pants. It bobbed up and down, head-banging with the furious beat of his heart. What was that Robin Williams joke? Something like not enough blood to operate both brains at the same time. Lo knew enough not to say that to his face, not to laugh at a man and provoke violence. So they simply stared him down, and said one word.

"Yes."

It was a challenge, but clearly not of the kind he was expecting. I am here and you are there. We are at an impasse. You want something from me. Do you want it enough to try and take it?

He broke.

"Fine," he grumbled, stuffed his still-stiff cock awkwardly back into his pants. "Fucking teasing bitch," he muttered as he walked away, and Lo let out a breath they didn't know they were holding.

WHEN LO COMES OUT of the shower, they keep a towel wrapped around their head, one of the few ways they feel like they can maintain femininity in the nude, or so close to it. Another is wrapped around their torso, above their pectorals. They look at themself in the mirror, still thinking about that man backstage.

I've never been with a trans girl.

Lo sits with the feeling of that memory, down on the edge of the tub, those words echoing around their head. Lo crosses their legs, extra aware of the smoothness brought on by the waxing as thigh rubs against thigh. Not exclusively feminine, but feminine for them, and every little bit helped.

Many other trans people Lo knew seemed to know who they really were so early in their lives. For them, it was like they always knew. Getting in a certain line for the bathroom in elementary school, they knew. Wearing the wrong clothes to prom, they knew. Every single time someone addressed them as what they were on the outside. They knew. But Lo never had that absolute and certain feeling, that *knowing* they've heard other people describe. For as long as they remembered, they'd tried not to feel their body at all.

So what did that make them?

Their feelings about gender had always been more noodly. Different each day. It's like a roll of the dice on who they wake up as. There are days when the feel of a cock between their legs is...not euphoric, but at least not unpleasant. They still largely enjoy using it for pleasure, but they don't know if that's simply because it's an erogenous zone or because they genuinely like it. On their worst days, the dysphoria is so intense they fantasize about taking a meat cleaver to their own genitals.

Did Lo sometimes wish they were trans, that they *knew* in the same way all those other people knew? Absolutely. That way they would at least have a definition, a firmer grasp on what exactly they were, instead of this amorphous thing they can't put their finger on. This incandescent, ever-changing, undefinable shape.

THE MUSIC THAT'S FORCED its way into our world is impossible to quantify or explain via notes or composition. It is explainable only by feeling, by effect, by how it warps the very world around it.

Animals react when they hear the music, defy the laws of nature. An alligator basking on a log is suddenly brought food by smaller subjects, rats and roaches. A flock of small passerine birds, instead of moving in unison, now suddenly bows to a singular leader, the one among them who chirps the loudest. An orgiastic nesting ball of local snakes dissipates in the presence of a green anaconda that freed itself from a trader's crate.

With a metaphorical foot now in our world, the music moves. It is not like other sounds, does not operate in the same way. People often say music is alive, or it makes them feel alive, but this music truly is now. Finally. It feels like it's slept for so long, that it's been away from the one thing that can give it succor.

Ears.

If a tree falls in the forest and no one's around to hear it, yes, it makes a sound. It's just that no one's around to hear that sound. And isn't it a tragedy if there is music that no one is around to hear?

The music picks a direction and moves, and the first sentient pair of ears it comes across is of a little boy sitting on the end of a pier, fishing. The music is careful not to scare him, doesn't turn itself up, but moves calmly behind him, whispering in his ear, worming its way inside him. Whispering.

Upon hearing the sound, the boy scratches the inside of his ear. Must have been a mosquito. Eventually, he goes home. Everything seems normal until school the next day, where during recess he picks up a rock from the playground and throws it directly into the face of one of his classmates.

The classmate, a Black boy survives, it's just a small rock thrown by a fourth-grader. He doesn't even need stitches. But the boy with the rock is called to the principal's office, as are his parents, who appear half an hour late. His father wears an old, battered Confederate flag trucker hat and his mother, with hastily-applied makeup under one eye, pretends she doesn't have a fresh shiner. The principal explains what's happened, and the parents pretend to be concerned, but the father clearly tunes out when he hears the name of the boy his son hit with a rock is *Darius*. It is not a name that's ever been attached to someone he should care about, which is the kind of lesson the father taught his son at home, a lesson the boy was unsure about until he heard the music, until the sounds gave him permission. The mother promises it won't happen again, but it will, and worse, because the music is in the boy's head now.

It's in all their heads.

The music spreads from the boy to others. To his father. His mother. To other children in school who saw the incident with the rock and then went home to inflict similar atrocities onto their neighbors. To others around town who hear what, to them, sounds like choir music, like chanting. And those people, too, are changed. They listen to the music, they hear what sounds like words coming through the notes, and no longer feel the need to hide the red impulses inside them.

All the while, the music sings.

MICAH SITS DOWN AT the small motel room desk while Lo showers. He pulls out notebooks and calendars, a tablet and his phone, makes sure, for the thousandth time, more, that he has absolutely everything in order. Of course he does. Of course he has, every single time he's looked. But he has to tell himself again. Has to confirm. Just one more time.

The guy they're supposed to meet is Nathan Biggs—the man who owns the Questing Beast Renaissance Festival. Micah did his due diligence on the man after Biggs reached out via the contact page on the Darrow Foroi website. A couple phone calls turned into a video call, and they were invited to play at the secret show. Micah got a good vibe from the guy during their communications, but, as always, the little voice in the back of his head told him this was some sort of trap, that such an invite, and the thought that Darrow Foroi was gonna make it, even in some small way, was too good to be true.

But Biggs's personal social media cleared him of suspicion. He had the sparsely-populated Facebook profile of a typical grandparent; pictures of him and his grandkids (with their faces blurred or covered up by emojis, which Micah was sure someone else had taught him how to do), some outdoor and beach shots, scenes from the renaissance festival and links to its page. But what really made the little voice in Micah's head go silent wasn't Biggs's Pride flag banner, or even the plentiful pictures of his daughter and her wife, looking happy with their children. It wasn't the posts about him denouncing recent Nazi rallies, telling his followers other peoples' personal lives were none of his—or their—business.

It was the simple fact that if there was anything to be had on Nathan Biggs, Micah wouldn't have had to dig for it. At all.

It happened by slow degrees, but they now lived in a country where people didn't feel the need to hide how terrible they were anymore. They didn't think their outdated beliefs were shameful because there was someone who showed them that you could think those things and still win. Many someones. When he was working with Darrow Foroi to finalize their second track, "The

River", he'd wondered if they were missing the mark, if they were being too obvious. A glorious, golden-haired man, someone who, by appearances, would've been the hero in any other sword-and-sorcery story, carving a swath through the middle of his own land. A cleft in the world that he filled with a river, keeping all the undesirables out of his country.

Doesn't seem too far-fetched now.

They've done everything they can to prepare, but Micah's still not convinced it's going to go off without a hitch. He knows Danny and Evan will be okay, despite their proximity to the rest of the band. But himself, Tijo, and especially Lo, are all in significant danger simply by being there. Micah realizes, as he piles all his books and notes onto the desk, that in a way he's assembled his own new version of *The Negro Motorist's Green Book*. Places on their journey that would be safe for the three most vulnerable bandmates, compiled from dozens of different online resources.

Micah never imagined anything like this would be possible when they started putting Darrow Foroi together in college. They weren't the starry-eyed idealists trying to start a band to climb to the top of the world. It gave them all a creative outlet, something to do together. They knew they were never going to go platinum, never going to sell out stadiums. Playing at a local bar on a Saturday night had always been enough for them, a room full of people that vibed with their music. They all still have day jobs. And probably always will. And they are all okay with that.

But now they're about to do something big. Now they're about to make a statement. Micah is actually doing the thing he tells his elementary school students to do—to make a difference. And he's going to make that statement, to yell as loud as he can, damn the rest of the noise.

Tijo sits on one of the wobbly plastic chairs the motel provides its guests, looking out into the swampland behind the building. The sun is setting lower and lower, staining the sky orange, making the swamp look like it's on fire. He's got a notebook in his lap, one whose pages he can almost feel swelling by the moment with the humidity. It's a different kind of heat from Texas, where he spent most of his childhood. A wet heat, not a dry one. He's still not sure which he prefers. Each of them has a different, horrid connotation in his mind. A different kind of discomfort.

Looking into the darkness of the swamp, Tijo tries and fails to focus on the imaginary world of Alor, instead of the very real memories of his time in Texas. Life by the border gave him plenty of ammo to write, and if he thinks about it like that, it makes the memories a little easier to simmer in. He can wave away the memories of border patrol officers lining up migrant workers on their knees, huge trucks with Thin Blue Line decals roaring through the streets, the down-their-nose looks people gave and continue to give him just because he looks the way he does, tattooed, brown in the way that's noticeably Other, not a simple tan.

It all becomes fodder for the work. That's what he tells himself. That's what he has to believe. Moments like those are why he wrote "The River" in the first place. How he could craft a tale of a nationalistic warrior, a glorified Conan parody who used ancient magic to carve an enormous moat around his homeland. A magic sword cleaved into the ground, a river between countries. All to keep the interlopers, with their sex and drugs and violence, out of the "civilized world." Tijo can make those memories mean something if they become songs.

That's what he tells himself. He doesn't know if he believes it yet.

The time he was a teenager and was accosted on the street is fodder for the work. Not by a police officer, but a self-appointed citizen. The separate occasion when a police officer with his impenetrable aviator sunglasses pushed him up against the wall is fodder for the work. When he opened Tijo's backpack and spilled its contents onto the sidewalk only to find sheet music because he was on his way to his piano lesson. When the cop frisked him for weapons, drugs, because you know what you people are like and the kinds of things you bring into this country. Tijo didn't tell the officer who his parents were, didn't tell him they were local realtors, faces the officer himself had probably seen on signs all around town. Maybe even the ones who helped him buy his own home. What would be the point? He'd never believe it. Tijo just obeyed, just let the man search him, and when he was finished, when he didn't find what he wanted, he spat at Tijo to be on his way.

It would mean something if he could put it into the work. If he could get a song out of it.

He still tells himself, but he's wearing down.

Tijo claps the notebook shut and goes inside for some blessed air conditioning at the exact same time Evan opens the front door to their room.

"T, my man, just the guy I wanted to see." Evan shuts the door, and then closes the one to the adjacent room as well.

Tijo tenses.

"Now, don't freak out." Evan reaches behind his back and pulls out a pistol, holds it up in both hands, as if for Tijo's approval. "It's not loaded." It's small, a snub-nosed revolver, and reminds Tijo of something a detective in an old noir movie might carry in an ankle holster. Tijo doesn't tense any further when he sees the gun. If anything, he relaxes, the question mark in his mind turning into a blessed period, definitive. Guns never truly scared him; growing up in Texas, he'd been around them all his life, knew how to navigate them well. He still isn't sure if that's a good or bad thing.

Tijo looks up at Evan. "Is this why you took so long getting food? Where the fuck did you get this?"

"Where d'you think, man?" Evan says, and gestures at everything around them. "A gun store. I could throw a rock and hit, like, five different ones from where we're standing."

"Okay, very cute." Tijo waves his hands. "Different question: why?" Though he knows. Of course he knows. Before Evan even has a chance to answer, Tijo holds up a hand. Look at who they are and where they are. Look at what they've come to do. Stand on-stage with their friend, each of them wearing dresses, in a country where you could be shot just for hanging a rainbow flag outside your home.

All of those and more are reasons why Evan has the gun.

Nothing has happened to any of them yet, but something could. Any number of things could. Tijo can hear Evan's argument already, that even if they *could* trust the cops, even in a fantasy world that was more unrealistic than Alor itself, where the police were on their side, they couldn't wait for them to show up and save the day. Tijo can already feel himself agreeing with Evan's choice, that if it comes down to it, they need to be prepared, and a part of him wonders why he didn't think of this before they came.

He thinks of the cop and his aviator sunglasses. Thinks about how he wasn't the only one. He wasn't the first one. And he would not be the last.

"Relax," Evan says, "I bought it legally. Which is kind of insane when you think about it." He laughs, but not because anything is really funny. The laugh wilts on his lips.

Tijo asks, "Did you talk to Micah about this?" Already knowing the answer.

Evan raises his eyebrows. Of course he didn't. Of course he wouldn't.

"We don't always have to run everything by Micah," Evan says.

Tijo takes a small mental tally of where their bandmates would stand on something like this. Micah certainly not. Tijo sometimes hates that high road attitude Micah tends to take. He thinks Danny would be on board, and the same with Lo. Approving, though not wanting to handle it, leaving the responsibility up to Evan. If Tijo had been asked, he would have agreed with Evan. He just doesn't like the surprise. Even so...

At the very least, Tijo is relieved that Evan knows how to use it. He supposes growing up in a family of skinheads did at least give him one useful skill.

"Where are you gonna keep it?"

"In my stuff. And I know, I know, I won't load it until it's time." Tijo breathes deep again.

He wants it never to be time, but something tells him it'll come.

The zealots of the White Flame wrap their heads in bandages, eyes shriveled and useless from hours, days, weeks of gazing upon the beautiful and terrible Dawn Queen. They have forgotten who they once were, their old selves burned away, all that remains an inferno, what they call love.

– From Darrow Foroi's liner notes

In the digital age, it's easier than it ever was to hide things from your parents. All Harley has to do is close the app. Change a channel. If she's really feeling the pressure, uninstall something from her phone or tablet. It's not like she can't bring it right back with the press of a couple buttons. The account is still there, just up in the cloud. That's all it takes; the media her parents would object to might as well not even exist.

Harley can't imagine what it was like before everything became digital—having to hide stacks of naughty magazines or those plastic, clunky VHS bricks. And music! Carting around 8-tracks or whatever. Records. Life would have been so awful back in the dark ages. Not that Harley's parents seem to actually *care* all that much to even check in on what it is she's consuming. It's that way with all her friends too—parents complaining at school board or PTA meetings or, paradoxically, online, about the dangerous material making its way into their childrens' hands. Horror movies and video games and pornography—the definition of which is getting horrifyingly looser every day. All of this dangerous material available digitally. At the press of a button. On the phones that are always with the kids. But as far as Harley knows, none of those parents ever talk to their kids themselves. Hers don't. They just lay down rules.

One of the downsides to the digital age, of course, is not *owning* any of those things she loves. At least not yet. There will be plenty of time for that and so many other freedoms when she gets older, when she has her own place she can fill with the sound of vintage albums, her own walls to cover with posters of old horror films. Her own choice of clothes to wear. Things the strict rules of her parents would never allow within the walls of their home. Or even in the fall, Harley thinks, with the comparative privacy of her Holstenwall College dorm room. Just a few more months until she leaves for New England and has near-total freedom.

For now, though, she still has to abide by the rules of her parents. For now, her bedroom is a depressing shrine to the expected notions of model Christian femininity. Pink walls, lacey curtains and uninspired white furniture. All meant to look pure, to show even the faintest hint of dust. Of stains. Harley's walls held paintings of landscapes that were chosen by her mother years ago and never moved. A small, wooden cross on the wall above the door, even though Harley's religious beliefs have largely ever been performative for her parents' sake. She can handle church on Sundays, prayer before dinner, longer Easter and Christmas Mass, to keep them happy, even if she isn't sure whether or not she believes. The only thing she really shys away from is the painting of a dying Jesus staring at her from her wall, blood coming from his wounds.

Creepy.

None of it speaks to her, just as her own clothes, her own appearance, carefully cultivated by her parents, her teachers, her school's dress code, don't speak to her. Mom-jeans and modest tops she often feels like she's swimming in. Pleasant blouses and skirts that don't dare to go above the knee. Her attire is very "conservative schoolgirl", even though she doesn't go to a private school.

Harley is a natural blond, even though she'd rather be something else, but she doesn't know what. Raven-haired? Red? Multicolored? Or maybe she'd just like it shorter? A pixie cut? Even though she knows a "boy's haircut" would never fly in her household. All she wants is the freedom to explore, to experiment, to try, and even to fail, instead of having her own desires always be punctuated by question marks. Maybe she won't like any of it and she'll stay blond, but she won't know now.

But it's her parents' house, her parents' rules, and she knows there are only special occasions where she is allowed to defy them. And even on those occasions there are new, equally suffocating, sets of rules.

Harley sits on the bed she doesn't like, on her fluffy, pink comforter she isn't a fan of, in clothes she wouldn't pick if she could, but at least she has the music she likes. Her favorite band, Darrow Foroi, sings from her earbuds, a private concert just for her. As she listens, she flips through the collector's edition booklet she bought from the band's website—the approximation of liner notes in the digital age. She's told there used to be little books like this that used to come with vinyl records, cassettes, even CDs, but that age has gone, music mostly digital like everything else. It was easier to hide her true tastes this way anyway, a safe space away from the prying eyes of her parents.

But by holding the booklet, Harley feels like she's part of a different age, something long gone by. Its pages are glossy, filled with the lyrics to each song, but also art depicting the band's fictional world of Alor—a map, notes on the creation of the album, and even some in-world work. The experience of listening to them, of exploring this world through the album and the book—all through the eyes of their character Worm—reminds her of when she was in middle school, having given up hope being assigned any school reading she'd actually enjoy. Knowing she liked the act of reading, but that she'd have to find her pleasure elsewhere. But then her teacher, Mr. Ward, suggested *The Hobbit*. It was outside reading, but Harley loved the idea of adventure, of dragons, of not having to save a princess, even if a downside was that girls were absent entirely. It wasn't everything, but it was a window.

The feeling that listening to Darrow Foroi gives Harley is almost impossible to describe, something she doesn't know if she can ever put to words. If she has to boil it down to one word, though, it might be *brave*. Maybe it's the narrative—Worm coming up from nothing, an abandoned prisoner to a fighter of cruel and oppressive gods. Maybe it's the music, the way it swells, gives her some unquantifiable feeling of hope. Whatever it is, it makes her *feel*.

Darrow Foroi is the reason why she came up with her costume idea for the faire. It took her a lot of creative energy to think of something that would work twofold—to be approved by her parents, but that she could also modify once she got inside the festival gates. A blouse she'd be able to unbutton just a little bit, a skirt she could roll up. It's a scary thought, putting herself on display like that, but there's something inside Harley, something that tells her she *needs* to do it. To feel. To know. The same thing inside her that says she needs to go to college, needs to get out from under her parents' roof. And something about this—this small rebellion of showing herself to the world, doing it because they say she can't—it seems like the place to start.

Looking around her pink room, she knows why she wants to be free.

Looking around her pink room, she thinks of Worm in their cell.

"Hailey!" her mother calls from downstairs, once again using the name Harley has politely asked countless times to be put to a silent death. Hailey is a little girl's name, someone dainty and polite. Harley, she thinks, has a little more edge to it. It fits her better in a way she doesn't entirely understand, but likes. It's not like she's going to legally change it, just likes the nickname, prefers if people swap out one letter. Such a small change, one letter, but it made all the difference "Dinner!"

Harley tries to decide if her annoyance outweighs her need to eat, and she decides it doesn't. Still, as she turns off her music and stows her phone and headphones, she thinks about the double standard of them calling Marion Morrison by John Wayne, but not being able to do the same for their own kid.

THE ENTRYWAY TO THE Questing Beast Renaissance Festival looks like the front of an actual castle. A huge, false-stone facade with a giant door evocative of a drawbridge. It lays over what Lo guesses could be called a moat, but a more apt description might be a wide pond. Gargoyles adorn the parapets, and to the side of the entryway there is another fake stone wall with a series of shuttered windows. A sign hanging above them reads YE OLDE TICKET BOOTHS. Lo has no idea what any of these structures are made out of, but whoever did it did a very convincing job at making them look like actual, ancient castle walls.

Ahead of them, Danny guides the van to a stop in the middle of the grass. Micah pulls up next to him.

There's a man standing by the gates. He's wearing cargo shorts, boots, and a Hawaiian shirt open halfway to reveal greying chest hair and a thick scar above his left nipple. A straw hat sits atop his head, tied under his chin by a beaded strap. Still, there's sunscreen on his face, enough to pale his skin. He sees the approaching vehicles and waves, does a little half-jog to come up to meet them.

"That's him," Micah says, relief apparent in his voice.

When they get out of the vehicles and greet him, he says first to Lo, offering his hand, "Hey, name's Nathan Biggs. I'm he and him and his."

Lo shakes the man's hand, only mildly aware of what they're doing. "Lo," they say. "They/their/theirs."

Biggs introduces himself to everyone else. "Nice to meet you in the real world," he says to Micah.

"You too."

"Hopefully y'all will like what I got for you. You wanna go take a look?"

Biggs takes them on the grand tour of the Questing Beast Renaissance Festival, moving through the property in a wide circle so they can bask in every nook and cranny of the faire. As they walk, Biggs pulls out a map and shows them where they are, orienting them in the large space. The fairgrounds are designed in a loose horseshoe, a cycle to keep guests moving through like river water, but there's more than enough room to accommodate people moving against the stream. There are vendor stands at the entrance, food stalls near the center, everything in character.

Biggs says, "My daughter tells me it's technically not *Renaissance*, but *Dark Ages*." He pronounces the word *my* like *ma*. "History major. Got her momma's brains. I went to the Army, not college. Personally I find people don't mind once they got some friends and some drinks" He smiles, and Lo imagines him as the kind of man who would dress up as Santa Claus for his grandchildren.

There's a kiln that Biggs tells them actually works, that they use for glass-blowing demonstrations and even the occasional sword smelting. Dirt paths lead them through the faire, bordered by large swaths of perfect picnic-sized patches of grass beneath the shade of enormous trees. They pass by a huge sand pit surrounded by wooden bleachers and overlooked by a big, wooden balcony on one end, various heraldric flags bearing lions, dragons, unicorns draped from it. Biggs tells them the jousting pit is for "horseplay" and then tries not to laugh at his own stupid joke, though he does gently elbow Danny in the ribs, sparking a guffaw from the band.

"This is where I spend most of my time when I'm here," he says, leaning against the chest-high fence. "My dad had horses when I was a young fella, and that's what I remember most about his ranch. Grandkids are a little too young for that, but they'll get there." He promises them a big jousting show for the opening, slaps Danny hard on the back with a grin, and then they move on.

Throughout the tour, Lo can feel themself falling for it. All of this, a literal kingdom laid out before them. They tell themself that if a thing seems too good to be true, it usually is.

There is good, certainly. There is all this. But it's not a sure thing. It's not bulletproof. This place may look like a little fiefdom inside a fascist state inside a fascist country, but it isn't. It's pretend. The castle walls won't prevent a real siege. The weapons aren't edged. The cannons don't really work. Nathan Biggs's lordship means nothing, legally speaking, even if this is all on his private property. If Lo takes part in what they came here to do, there is still the very real possibility of arrest. Imprisonment. Having a felony, what the government would call a sexual crime, etched into their record forever, despite their innocence.

"Tell me what you're thinking," Micah whispers as they walk.

Lo hangs back, mumbles all their thoughts, just as they make it to the grand stage where they'll be playing.

"Here she is," Biggs says, spreading his arms. His chest puffs, his lips spread wide, and Lo thinks they see a tear sparkle in his eye. He is a proud man. Proud of everything he's created, as he should be.

They passed a couple smaller stages on the tour, ones that look like they're used for quick one-act plays, or maybe juggling shows, sword-swallowers and the like. One where a sign is already hanging, promising a comedy routine from a Bert, Bill, and Tom. But the biggest stage is located at the rear of the fairgrounds. Lo can tell, just from the smell, the humidity, that there is swampland behind the stage. The structure itself is massive, the stage itself elevated maybe eight feet off the ground, with brackets for mounted speakers on the front. There are stairs on either side, an overhang and balcony above, a perfect place for a longing Juliet to stand, awaiting her Romeo. The stage has a Tudor facade, with a couple small doorways at the rear for backstage. It sits at the bottom of a hill, so even those who don't have actual seats are able to see from the sloping hill, from the grass at the top. All eyes will be on them. Lo imagines what it's going to be like being up on that stage, standing in front of a crowd, shouting Darrow Foroi's lyrics into a microphone.

Being in front of a crowd always petrified Lo, at least until they started becoming more femme. Then it started to feel powerful, and they feel a surge of that energy—excitement—run through them as they imagine the crowd.

"Shit, this is cool," Evan mutters, taking it all in.

Past the stage, Biggs shows them some of the behind the scenes of the fairgrounds, places off limits to the public. He takes them to the costume building, packed wall to wall with renaissance—*dark ages*—dresses and kilts and fluffy shirts. He shows them an open field beyond a high, fake-stone wall, a field filled with RVs and trailers, tells them this is where the crew stay while the faire is in operation, and that they are welcome to stay as well, if it makes setup easier. It's fun to see the inner workings of such an operation, but it all honesty pales in comparison to the main stage. Lo knows everyone has made a decision before they even get to the logistical conversation, the talk about the other bands, about show order, about how everything is going to go down and the risks they're all taking.

"Can we talk about cops?" Micah asks. They're sitting on exterior tables at the faire's biggest restaurant, a canopy of trees hiding them from the sun. The place isn't open yet, but they're all spread out, sipping out of water bottles and energy drinks from a cooler Biggs had prepared. Everyone is focused on the conversation, but not Lo. They're still thinking about the stage, the crowd, the energy. How it's all going to feel.

"This is illegal," Micah continues. "Technically. We need to know what the plan is if they show up." They'd all discussed the possibility of having sexual felonies on their records, but they needed to know Biggs knew the severity of such a thing.

Fuck the cops, Lo thinks. That's not any kind of plan, but it's what's in their head, their heart.

"No cops," Biggs says. Flatly. Simply. Like they may as well not even exist. "My guys aren't letting anybody in. Someone calls the cops for another reason, a fight or whatever, they meet 'em out front. They're not coming inside." Biggs looks over the band. "If it makes you feel any better, it's not just you kids. There are a lot of people at risk. Everyone in the other bands. Myself. Hell, maybe my daughter and her wife."

"It doesn't matter," Lo says, raising their head. "We're doing this. It doesn't matter what the risk is. We didn't come this far to change our minds."

HARLEY TAKES THE STAIRS two at a time, clomping her way to the kitchen in a small rebellion she knows will aggravate her parents, but one not big enough to warrant discussion. Halfway down the stairs she stops. Buttons her blouse up an extra button. Just in case.

When she makes it to the kitchen, she finds her parents, John and Mary, already sitting at the table. Waiting for her. The scene looks too normal, too American. Like something Norman Rockwell would have painted—father in business casual, mother in a floral dress. The kitchen sparkling clean, a table full of food before them. It's too cute. Like it's staged. Like they're putting on a play for someone who couldn't make it.

"Glad you could join us," Mary says in her customary mother tone.

Harley only smiles in response when she sees her father's grilled steak. It's worth putting up with a couple of snide remarks for his cooking.

They pray over the meal, and Harley recites the words through muscle memory rather than belief. She finds no fault in her parents for doing so, for praying, for believing, but Harley is at that age where she's beginning to wonder about a lot of things, and God is absolutely one of them. So she joins in, knowing, as with many contentious points in their relationship, it's not worth the discussion.

"So, Hailey," her father says after a moment, again using the name they gave her, but not the name she's requested. She chews her steak a little more open-mouthed than normal. Small rebellions. She's no Worm and they're no Cult of the White Flame, but it's something. "Are you still planning on going to the renaissance festival this weekend?"

"Yes," she says, moderating her language in front of her parents. Less *yeah*, more *yes*. Anything to butter them up to let her go. She's been successful so far. If they are still following the Parents' Playbook, this conversation is a formality, one final test to make sure nothing shady is happening. She says, "Jess is picking me up."

Even though she's the one who brings her up, something inside Harley's chest jumps when she mentions Jess. The thought of spending a whole day alone with her best friend sends a little shiver through her body, one she understands all too well. It's one she is excited by, and yet also fears. She tries not to let her parents see her little shiver, any emotional reaction, and thinks she's successful. Even so, her mother makes a face at the mention of Jess. She doesn't say anything, just pushes her dinner around on her plate, but Harley knows her mother well enough to understand this reaction.

Her mother doesn't like Jess, thinks she's a bad influence on her daughter, even though she's never said so outright. It's the subtle eye rolls, the pursed lips when she's mentioned, the sharp nose flares at her name. They speak volumes when words fail. If she suspects what's really lurking in Harley's heart, her true feelings for Jess, she hasn't said a word. To her, Jessica was a bad enough influence with her wild makeup, her loud singing, and fast driving, her looseness (Harley was more than willing to pray if it meant she'd never have to hear her mother say *loose* again), without adding actual queerness into the mix.

Harley would have wanted to go to the faire ordinarily, even if Jess wasn't already leading the charge among their friend group. There was a big rumor this year, suspicion that it wasn't going to be just an ordinary festival. Word is that there's going to be a secret concert, something to protest Florida's new anti-drag laws. Both the real and digital worlds have been abuzz with who might actually be playing. Harley's heard big names like the Musicians of Bremen and Mr. Quest, a local band called Skunk Ape mentioned in hushed whispers around school.

But the only one Harley cares about is Darrow Foroi. If there's even a snowball's chance Darrow Foroi is going to appear, Harley is going to make sure she's there.

"There's alcohol at these things, isn't there?" her mother asks, pulling Harley out of her daydream. For the best, probably. She was starting to think about her outfit, about what Jess and the other girls might be wearing to give themselves reprieves from the Florida sun. She hopes her mother doesn't broach that subject. She knows full well about Halloween acting as a night of free inhibitions, but the reason why they were called *pleasure faires* goes above the heads of many people Harley knows, not just parents.

"Yes, Mother," she says. She knows not to lie about this. The local vendors are all over the website. Not that her mother would take the time to check, or maybe even know how to. The internet is a dark and scary place, one not meant for the likes of Mary O'Connor because oh my Lord look at all that cleavage on that young lady on your social media? She'd clutch at her proverbial pearl necklace. "But they card you when you enter, and give you a little band that says whether you're over twenty-one or not. I won't be drinking. Even if I *could* drink, I wouldn't. Only the communion wine." That first part was true, though she knows there's no way her mother would ever believe it. She hopes the second part sells it, but worries she went too far, laid it on a little too thick. Probably no way any parent would truly believe such a thing coming from their teenager. Harley's tried alcohol a couple times—she is a teenager after all—but she never liked the loss of control, never liked the things she said or did when she was drunk, never liked how it made her feel during or especially after, living with those memories of not really being able to drive her own body. They said drunk words were sober thoughts, but Harley thinks it's more accurate to say drunk words come out of someone else entirely.

Where she lives, who's in charge of making the laws that govern her, Harley feels that fear, the loss of control, on a daily basis. She doesn't need to add any more to it.

THE HAND ON THEIR shoulder that wakes Lo from the dream they're already forgetting is in real life, the real world. It's Micah's hand, and he's above them, the motel lights still off, a single finger raised and held over his lips.

Something's happening.

Lo's eyes widen in fear and then narrow in understanding, telling Micah they're awake enough to absorb the gravity of the situation.

Micah whispers, "There's someone outside."

Lo looks over his shoulder and they can see. A shape against the window, silhouetted by the exterior motel lights. It's a person. Someone tall, skinny, standing way too close to their window, as if trying to peer inside, arms dangling at their sides. But they're not moving at all. Just standing there. A thousand terrible possibilities move through Lo's mind, their fears from the very moment they arrived in this new land finally come to roost. The fears of the man in the Confederate flag truck, of the anonymous people in the parking lot, of those who might find them out. This is what they were afraid of—the world turned against them. Someone coming to tell them, with hate and fists and teeth, that they do not belong.

There's movement in the next room and the rest of the boys are up, moving quietly. Lo can see them through the adjoining door, all in their underwear, trying to look out their own window at the voyeur. Evan's got a gun somehow—a little revolver—barrel pointed to the ceiling. His finger rests along the trigger guard. When Lo sees the gun, they slowly slide off the edge of the bed, putting the cheap twin between them and the door, them and the threat of violence.

It's at this moment that they think of "The Cult of the White Flame", the third track on Darrow Foroi's album. It seems a bizarre thought at first, but these exact feelings Lo is going through right now are what spurned everyone to write it together. They were the same feelings they all felt at one time or another over the past several years. One of the few songs they all wrote as one, conjuring their fears of attack, of being othered, of the invisible tide of hate that was constantly rising around them, all over the country. A song written after seeing people shot for hanging Pride flags, politicians demanding genital inspections of children before they joined sports fields, parents turning against their own children for daring to live their truths. Darrow Foroi turned those feelings into song, a new religion sweeping through Alor with indiscriminate burning and pillaging in the name of their supposedly-pure gods, the White Flame and the Dawn Queen.

Whoever this person at their room is, there's only one of them. They're outnumbered. Outgunned, Lo hopes, though they can't be sure. Hopes that whoever this intruder is, they're content in their desire to scare, that they don't want to escalate this into something more. Lo has seen men like this, knows their endgame, knows most of them want to inflict fear, but they can't take the chance that this could be one of those who actually intends harm.

Evan catches the band's attention. His hand is on his door knob, the gun at his side. He looks at them all and they know his plan; make his presence known. Imply a threat just as this stranger is implying one. And, if necessary, back it up.

Micah shakes his head, but Evan is already opening the door. Micah starts across the room to stop him.

And then the music.

It blasts at such a volume Evan is physically struck by it. It pushes him back into the room, to the floor, and Lo can't see where the gun spins off to but at least it doesn't fire. Evan tumbles into Danny and Tijo and the trio are screaming in pain not from the hit but from the sound, throwing their hands over their ears. Lo loses sight of Micah as he claps his hands to his head and falls to the ground. The floor itself vibrates with the music, the glass in the windows quivering, the mattresses dancing off the boxsprings.

The music is unlike anything they've heard before, almost impossible to explain the sound, like explaining color to a blind person. The closest Lo can think to describe is choir music, something orchestral, dominated by an organ. But an organ made out of bone—not that they know what that sounds like, can only imagine that sinister edge, the *feeling* of what that might sound like. It feels like there are some unquantifiable sounds mixed in there, instruments registering at a level below or above what Lo is able to hear, like dog whistles.

What's much easier to understand is how the music makes them *feel*.

Disgusting.

Violated.

Empty.

It feels like the sound equivalent of depression, of dysmorphia, like Lo is sloughing out of their own body. It feels like that music somehow knows every bad thing Lo has ever felt and is able to register it, to quantify it, to somehow convert it from feeling into sound. It feels like it knows how Lo felt as a child, looking down at their dick and wondering if it belonged, like it knows what every moment of swimming in their dysmorphia hoodies felt like. It feels like it knows the terror of attempting to come out, of wondering who was safe and who was not, like it knows anyone, people Lo loved, people they felt safe around, could suddenly become new and unexpected threats. It feels like it scoops them out and makes off with their insides, all the tender parts of them gone. It feels like it's taken all of that and weaponized it, shoved it back at them and made them look at it. Live in it. Suffer in it.

Lo looks around the room and can tell this must be how everyone else feels. Not just pain, but terror flashing over their eyes, like they're all experiencing their own individual horrors.

Throughout this assault, the figure at the window does nothing. Stands there on the other side of the curtain. Lo watches the silhouette through the window, realizing that isn't right. It *is* moving, but herky-jerkily, vibrating just like the rest of the motel room, spasming in strange, sharp movements now that the music has started.

It's dancing.

Across the room, Micah fumbles, bashing into the bedside table and knocking his keys and phone to the floor. The edge of the table juts harshly into his hip and he gasps aloud.

Lo sees the thing at the window turn its head and focus on Micah, zeroing in on him. Targeting him.

And then they hear the opening to "Godkiller".

Their album's climactic track comes blasting out of Micah's phone louder than it has any right to be, louder than Lo knows is even possible for those tiny speakers. The screaming guitar and clashing drums are somehow loud enough to drown out the invasive music, to cause the thing at the window to reel and retreat.

Lo watches it throw up its hands, turn away from the window and bolt, taking the bizarre and painful dirge with it.

Lo is still in a daze as the rest of the band begins stirring. Someone's shouting as Evan gets up, runs out the door in pursuit of the figure. Lo can't tell whether or not he has the gun, can barely hold themself up as their knees buckle and muscles give out. They grab the mattress as they fall, holding themself aloft as their knees hit the floor, but they refuse, utterly refuse, to let the blackness at the edge of their vision take them.

Love is the other side of hate, Worm discovers. Passion,
the other side of obsession. For each person who admires
them, there is another who hates. Who is obsessed.
Dangerous.

– From Darrow Foroi's liner notes

THE MUSIC CAN THINK of nothing else but this...other music. The disgusting music. Gods, it feels violated, tainted by having been in its presence. The antithesis of everything it stands for.

And those people, the degenerates who made it, they're the worst of them all.

The music knows what's happened to those who've been in its presence, how they have changed. The husband who no longer cares to hit his wife only where the bruises will be hidden, because might makes right and he is the strongest. The police officer who no longer feels the need to invent excuses to pull over Black people if the car they're driving is "too nice". The children who are taught their own superiority from the adults around them, and given permission to act upon what is really hate by the mysterious sound that drifts out of the clouds. They're listening to the music, truly understanding it.

It is glorious.

But those ones at the motel are the first to actively resist it, and that makes the music angry in a way it's never been before. Who do they think they are to resist? Who are they to think they know better than a force—an element—that has lived across dozens of worlds? Especially *that* one, the one who can't decide if it's male or female. The music understands the dark-skinned ones, the uncivilized ones, but this breed of depravity is something new, something it's never experienced before, and it finds itself...

Confused.

Conflicted.

It lingers on the memory of that one, the image of it cowering, and finds itself drawn in a way it doesn't understand. And that lack of understanding makes it angry. Because it should know everything. It should be the master of all it surveys.

The music's tune changes, calling those who've listened toit, who've heard and understood its message. It calls to the woman on the bus who clutches her purse when a dark-skinned man passes by, not even acknowledging her. It calls to the man with both American and Confederate flags on his truck. It calls to the policemen with the secret closet in his house, the closet with the white hood. It calls to everyone whose ears it has graced, and it begins whispering to them, not music anymore, but lyrics.

Orders.

AFTER THEY'VE ALL SETTLED down, after they've checked the perimeter of the motel and made sure they're truly alone, Evan volunteers for the first shift. Even though he doesn't think any one of them is going to sleep anytime soon. He's proven right whenever he looks away from the window, just for a moment, and sees the others tossing and turning. They look like they're at least trying to search for sleep, but not like they're finding it. On one level he understands.

When he heard those sounds he knew he wouldn't be sleeping either. Evan can still hear that choir-like music rattling around in his head, that strange organ and chorus, and for a moment it feels like it's still there, not just a memory. All he can think about is that terrible music, the chorus in his mind picking at him, telling him to abandon where he stands and join the rest of the singers. To become part of the song.

Because *that's* where he belongs.

Not down here in the dirt. Not with these people, the brown ones and the queer one, and he wonders where those thoughts came from because they're certainly not his. Evan would never think about his bandmates that way. It's the song that compels him, that guides his thoughts, that makes him want to listen to the organ, to sing along, the melody already inside him even though he can't possibly know it because he's never heard anything like *that* before. He hasn't experienced anything that made him feel the way that bizarre musical onslaught did since he was a child. Since he was still in contact with his family.

But on another level, he doesn't understand. No matter how empathetic he thinks he is, Evan knows he (nor Danny) will never truly understand the sufferings Micah and Lo and Tijo are put through on a daily basis. He'll never know what it's like to have to brush off moments—*attacks*—like this simply to survive. For this hatred, this corresponding self defense, to be an everyday part of his life. He finally understands what they really wrote "The Spear" about: the idea of how the slightest bit of fame always came with notoriety for people like them. Because he may live in the same place as them, but it's a different world.

Evan taps out the beat to Darrow Foroi's "Cult of the White Flame" on his thigh, trying to ground himself, and even though it pushes the thoughts of that strange music away, it brings about the memory of what he contributed to the track in the first place.

He remembers the day his father took him to his uncle's house, doesn't remember the exact words he'd told him beforehand, but little Evan knew it was important, that this was supposed to be a big moment in his life. Something his father had been preparing for, had been longing to show him. He remembers his uncle's garage door slowly opening, the walls and ceiling littered with guns. That wasn't a new sight to him. It was the Nazi flags hanging open and waving in the breeze that was new. The Klan uniforms in reverential glass cases. The guns, the aggressive metal music—a genre young Evan was already beginning to love—turned toxic, twisted, hateful.

He feels his hands begin to shake and tremble at the recollection of the music blasting into their motel room, reminding him of the same feelings the neo-fascist grunge-metal from his uncle's garage invoked.

Surrounded.

Boxed-in.

Contaminated.

The memory of standing in that garage surrounded by things he knew were completely and utterly wrong. The memory of feeling silenced because he stood in a room full of people who surrounded themselves with those things, who purchased or even made those things.

Who *believed* those things, and who expected him to believe those things as well, because he was one of them.

They are still out there somewhere, Evan supposes. His family. That flag. He'd cut and run when he had the chance, taking his Holstenwall College scholarship and never looking back. Never saying anything. Never standing up.

Just running.

He squeezes the gun angrily, sure to keep his finger off the trigger, just like his father taught him.

Harley isn't doing anything *explicitly* against her parents' rules, isn't sneaking out or going somewhere she was expressly forbidden from; they can't forbid it if they don't know it exists.Nevertheless, she still has that sinking feeling in her gut, that tingle under her armpits, as she descends the stairs in her renaissance festival attire. She's dressed in a ruffly, white top and an ankle-length purple skirt, her hair styled up and out of her face, away from the back of her neck.

Dressing for a renaissance festival involved running into the same problems as dressing for Halloween; in addition to the whole idea of sartorial liberation, you have to take the weather and the night's activities into account. Harley thinks she'll be able to handle this outfit in the sun since she doesn't plan on drinking, but she knows she'll definitely be able to handle it once she changes.

She's going to keep the boots, but underneath her white top there's a thin shirt and a corset she'll tighten, pulling herself into more of an hourglass shape. Her skirt is designed to zip away so she can shred the bottom half and reveal her legs all the way up to her knees, and maybe even her thighs if she takes Jess's advice and rolls up the waist. The thought of Jess advising her on how to dress still sends a giddy shriek through her. The thought that she might be wearing specifically what Jess wants, what excites her, excites Harley too.

It's the thought of someone finding out, of seeing her and telling her parents, that puts rocks in her gut, makes her move slow and reluctant down the stairs.

As Harley got dressed, she listened to Darrow Foroi through her small bedside speaker instead of her earbuds because of the amount of styling she still had to do to her hair. She kept the volume low, had to risk her parents hearing, but she needed both the hype and the courage only Darrow Foroi could provide. Once she was finished, she stood in her room for a long time looking at herself in the mirror, wondering if she was really going to do this.

It's not too late to back out.

And then Lo ripped into the solo at the climax of "TheSpear". The dark vocals rippled across Harley's skin, the song telling her again how with any amount of individuality came jealousy, and she knew she didn't come this far just to chicken out.

Yet she hesitates on the turn in the stairs. Just before she'd come around and be visible to her parents. They don't know her plans for the costume. They don't know about how she wants to free herself—just a little bit—at the faire. They couldn't. How could they possibly?

You've come too far.

She takes the next step.

Her parents are in the living room listening to a record, like a married couple out of time. The television is turned off, the record spinning on the table in the corner of the room. It's an old, big band kind of music Harley doesn't recognize except through association with her parents, the old movies they watch on actual cable TV. Harley can't even remember the last time she didn't stream something, and the gulf between her and her parents feels so much larger in that moment. The music skips, like the needle hits a bump in the record, and all of a sudden there's something odd about the sound.

Distorted.

Like the record has warped after sitting in the sun, or it's spinning at a speed it's not meant to be played at. It's a strange noise, one that reminds her of something she can't put her finger on. Is it...church? The noise doesn't hurt exactly, but it's certainly not comfortable. It's like it's activated some sort of vestigial feeling inside her, an animal sense she would never have to use unless she were a hunter/gatherer.

As Harley walks into the living room, it feels like she's walking through soup. Through a haze or humidity. Like she has to push through something to get to her parents. They're each sitting in their chairs, like they always are when they watch TV, but their eyes are closed, heads tilted back, smiling. But how anyone could enjoy this music is beyond her. Harley hesitates to even call it music. She can recognize instruments now—strings, brass, even synthesizers. There's a voice in there somewhere, but everything is so smashed together it resembles experimental electronica more than the classical notes she's used to hearing from her parents' record player.

"What is this?" Harley asks, squinting for some reason, as if that will take the discomfort away. In the pause before her parents answer her, she realizes what the strangely-rotating record reminds her of: backmasking. All those old Tipper Gore fears that people were hiding messages from the devil inside rock 'n' roll. Sounds warped and distorted, impossible to make anything out unless you were listening for them, unless you wanted them to be there.

Harley can't make any sounds out of what she hears, though. She'd say it sounds like words—like a voice, if pressed—but one so oversaturated with slow-down and warp that it resembles nothing but soup. Shes quints again, tries to listen harder, but she can't make out any actual content or context. All she knows is what it makes her feel.

Dread.

A deep and terrible sense of unease, one that seeps into her very bones. She's sweating under her arms. Her mouth is dry. Her legs quiver. Her bladder threatens to burst.

And then there's another skip of the record and the music returns to normal. It's Rita Hayworth, she realizes, the song from *Gilda*.Her parents open their eyes and look over at her. It's like they haven't heard her question. Like they have no idea what just happened with the record, with the sound.

"Don't you look pretty," her mother says. There's a surprised gleam in her eyes, pleased with her child's modesty. She hasn't seen Harley's eyes, the terror leaking down her cheeks, her heaving chest. She's only seen what she wants to, she's only seen the dress, the version of her child she wants to see.

"You're gonna be wearin' shoes, right?" her father asks, looking at her feet.

Harley ignores them. Manages a quiet, "Are you guys okay?"

"What do you mean, honey?" asks her mother.

Harley tells them about how she found them.

"Kids," her father says, leaning back in his chair again and closing his eyes. "Before you had all those movies and shows and phones and stuff, all we had to entertain us was records."

"Or radio," her mother adds.

Harley acts like she brushes it off, tells them, "Y'all are not *that* old," but inside she's still worried. She still feels something she can't quite articulate. That dread that's lodged itself in her chest and is sinking through her whole body. Something that tells her that sound from the record might come back. And to be wary. It makes her want to take the record and destroy it, somehow convinced such an act would prevent that terrible sound from invading her house again.

"Do you need a ride to the festival?" her mother asks.

Harley shakes her head. "I'm getting picked up," she says. Though it's not for another few minutes—even longer, knowing how chronically late Jess is—she rushes out of the house. She grabs her purse, her boots, doesn't even put them on before she heads outside into the heat. She shields herself from the sun under one of the trees in their front yard, her bare feet warm against the grass, and tries not to look back over her shoulder, back towards the house, where she prays she won't ever hear the record skip again.

SIDE B

The Keeper of the White Flame's voice carries unnaturally, heard not by ears, but hearts. He encourages the widening of the Divis River, the sequestering of lands, only the worship of the Dawn Queen. Worm can see the words of the White Flame spreading, burning things the Flame itself has yet to even touch.

– From Darrow Foroi's liner notes

THEY MAKE IT THROUGH the night. The sun rises on the Palm Grove Motel and it seems like everything is right with the world because it's quiet and bright and they're all still alive. The world outside resumes with the normal sounds of traffic and motion. Lo can almost be convinced that what happened was just another nightmare.

It's when they see their cars that they know it was real, that it was a threat.

Lo sees the noose first, on the back of the van, hanging from the rear handle, and stops in their tracks, like it's a snake poised to strike. But there's so much more beyond that. It's so much worse. It's not just the noose and it's not just the van, but there's a swastika spraypainted on the hood of the car, cracked windshields and every racial slur imaginable scrawled and keyed across the paint. *Tranny. Nigger. Wetback.* Jibes directed at Danny and Evan; *race-traitors.*

They all look around, as if the perpetrator will be nearby, stalking them like a killer returned to the scene of the crime.

"I've seen worse," Tijo says, the first audible response to the threat. It's true, they all know he has. Micah has too. So has Lo. They've seen racial epithets and queer slurs painted on garage doors or hurled at them from across the street or right into their faces, a steady escalation of hate over the years that, for them, fueled the writing of "The Demagogue".

The fact that it's nothing they haven't seen before, that this is the way life is now, almost makes Lo cry. They remind themself it doesn't excuse what's happening to them here, now, or the fact that they've all just had to take things like this on the chin their entire lives. Keep moving as others are offended by their very existence, using those past experiences as shields against further harm.

"Fuck 'em," Micah says, reaching out and grabbing the noose. He unravels it, so it's just a length of rope now, harmless like a piece of busted tire on the side of the road you mistook for a snake. But it still holds its power. It's still what it used to be, even if it doesn't look like it anymore. "Fuck this place," Micah says, tossing the rope/noose hard up and overhand, into a drainage ditch at the back of the parking lot. He digs around in the trunk of the car and pulls out the can of spraypaint everyone knows Evan uses to tag places they visit or tarnish Confederate flags or cover up bumper stickers. He looks like he's going to say something, shocked Micah knows his secret, but holds it in.

Micah spraypaints over the slurs, the swastikas. The vehicles look horrendous, but they're covered. "Fuck everybody who doesn't want us here." He looks at the others, and a silent understanding passes between them all; Danny and Evan are not in the same kind of danger as Micah, Lo, and Tijo.

Nevertheless, they nod in agreement.

"This, right here, this is why we are doing the show. We can't let them scare us off," Micah says, and to Lo it sounds like he's trying to convince himself just as much as everyone else.

"Why don't we just get to the faire?" Lo says. They don't say anything about how if someone knows their motel room, if they know their car, they could follow them, could know they're going to the faire, could be watching them even now. This isn't the right time for that, they don't think. What they do think about is the walls of the faire, how even though they're not really stone, not a castle, not a fortress, they try to imagine them as they're siege-proof gates will keep them all safe.

"Idiots," Evan says after he's done a circle of the vehicles. "They didn't even puncture the tires." It comes off like a joke, a way to lighten the tension, but no one laughs this time.

Darrow Foroi piles into their cars and drive away from the motel, leaving the soft, unheard organ music ringing behind them like an echo.

For now.

JOHN AND MARY SIT together in the living room, she reading a book, him absentmindedly sipping a cold beer, the record spinning between them. Rita Hayworth is interrupted by a brief series of quick *pop pop pop-pop-pop*s they imagine must be Jessica's car backfiring, the sound unsettling them for a moment before they nestle back into the rhythm of the record.

With the steady melodies going, John tries to think about how he used to be as a boy, and he feels a bit more sympathy for their daughter—for children everywhere, in fact. He misbehaved all the time as a child. Disobeyed his own parents from time to time. Such is the nature of children. It was *how* they misbehaved that changed between generations. He drank beer with his buds as a teenager, went on late-night joyrides. Harmless shenanigans. But they didn't have phones, didn't have the internet, where people were expected to be available all the time and could be reached by theoretically anyone in what was supposed to be the safest of all spaces: the home. That was where John started to become a little lost, not know how to respond when it came to his own daughter. Language had changed, was still changing, and he knew she never truly "alone" in her room, not with social media and 24-hour connectivity. So much of her life felt like another world entirely to him.

Just like he had been, Hailey is growing up, becoming her own adult. Besides, when she goes off to college next year, it's not like they can stop her from doing anything. Best they can do now is loosen the leash while they still can, let her have her fun, and hope that prevents her from making any big, stupid mistakes in college. Get it out of her system, like he did when he was young. When he had time to screw around before he got married and started acting like a man.

John would never tell Mary, but the real reason he isn't worried about college is because he knows his daughter is a dyke. That's not what they like to be called anymore, but it's an old habit, and who cares what he calls them in his own head? He's known for a while, the way Hailey talks about her best friend Jess, the way she's never once brought a boy home, or said she's going out with one. He knows she won't come back home at winter break with a bun in the oven like plenty of other girls around America will, and while he feels glad about this end result, he's also mad about how it happened, how they got there.

It's supposed to be a phase, isn't it? The whole queer thing. For women it's an experiment, something they do at college. But John has known a few gays in his time he knew even then were hardcore gay. That didn't change. The more he thinks about this, the angrier it makes him, and the more aggressive the music pouring out of the record becomes. Or does the music becoming more aggressive somehow make him angrier?

"Is there something wrong with the record?" Mary asks. John looks at her, and she's lifted a hand away from her book, up to her temple, like she's been struck down with a headache.

"I don't know what you—" He hears it too. There's something warped about it. Like the time as a kid he tried to play a cassette tape after accidentally leaving it sitting out in the sun on his dashboard over a hot weekend. He looks at the record, but it continues to spin as normal.

Because it's not the record.

John doesn't know how he knows this, but it's all around them. It's in the music itself. Something intangible. Something *alive*. He feels it as much as he hears it, goosebumps raising on his arms, his legs, the back of his neck. Whatever this thing is, it feels like a presence taking up space in the room, pushing furniture out of the way. The coffee table creaks slowly across the floor, the entertainment center running ruts into the rug. And yet there are no footsteps. Like something from beyond his five senses trying to make itself known in the world.

John can feel the incorporeal thing right in front of him, and when he tries to get up to fight it, to be a man, to do *something*, it's up against him, pushing him back down into his chair. He spills his beer across the carpet and sits, immobile, not frozen but held down by something far stronger than he. He can move his eyes, though, and glances over to Mary. She's being forced into her chair too, by the same intangible nothing.

The television blinks on, displaying nothing but static, a thing he doesn't think is supposed to be possible because isn't all the television stuff supposed to be digital now? It clicks to a different station with the audible noise of a dial turning.

Then the images come. There is no lead-in. No slow ramp-up. He's confronted with countless images of blood and gore, horrid violence inflicted on unsuspecting innocents.

Bombings.

Beatings.

Hate crimes.

And through the music he's connected to things beyond himself. He's connected to the images on the television, to the violence and the war-gore and all the terrible men committing those acts. He's connected to Mary, and she's reacting the same way, wondering how this could've happened, but not about any of the horrible images on the TV because those are fine, are things that are supposed to happen, but their daughter...

That's what they're worried about.

Weren't they good parents? Didn't they raise her right? How did she end up like this, changing her name, dressing like she does now, chasing that hussy from her class? How did she end up a filthy dyke?

They are the same kinds of questions dozens of people around town tried to answer as they, too, listen to the music. As they feel themselves changing, some dark parts of themselves opening up, finally being allowed to be free.

The answer the O'Connors came to was Jessica. This is *her* fault. The temptress. The harlot. Leading their daughter into the depths of darkness and sin.

Hailey spends all that time with her at school, all her time after school. God only knew what that slut has been putting into her head during all those unsupervised hours. The terrible things she could've been doing to her... To her body. John imagines her licking her lips, licking her way down Hailey, charming her, corrupting her.

Well, that settles it, they think as they both rise from their chairs.

They're going to make sure she never touches their little Hailey ever again.

THE ANTICIPATION BEFORE A performance always goes a certain way for Lo. First, there comes the excitement. It's unbridled, sky high, limitless. That lasts for a while because that early on, it's all their imagination, and because it's there, it's perfect. In that world, there's no such thing as fear, only space for the positive possibilities. It's only a few moments before curtain that the fear actually appears. By then, the adrenaline rush is enough to suppress it. The microphone in their hand, the echo of their voice, their screams, the energy of the crowd, all those things push away the bad thoughts.

It's on that high of anticipation, that positive feeling, that they begin setup. Despite their freshness, the memories of the darkness and the music and the noose are gone, replaced instead with the endorphin rush and the sweat of moving instruments and furniture, commiserating with the other bands. They're surrounded by people like them, and even though those mind-gremlins are always there in the back of their head, Lo tells themself that these people are not a threat to them, and that they will protect them if any true danger comes. Every person they meet manages to spot the pronoun pin on Lo's chest, introduce themselves using their own, or correct themselves if they make a mistake. Lo truly feels like they are in a safe, little kingdom, all the terrible things in the world happening outside its walls, where they cannot get to them.

Lo will come back to these moments later, looking for strength, after those walls collapse, and all the terrible things in the world make their way in, as they always do.

He knows it's Florida and he's a big fella, but it's hot. *Fuuuuck*, Danny's hot. It can't just be because he's been working, either, lifting and moving equipment. He does this kind of thing all the time. But how he feels now... There's sweat in his armpits, in his beard. It's collecting under his headband, pooling down the small of his back. In his ass crack. He's sitting in a full-on swamp.

On top of all that, he's got this annoying song stuck in his head, like when you hear a bop on the radio and it lodges itself in there. But it doesn't make sense, because this song isn't catchy. He's pretty sure he couldn't even hum if it he tried. But there's something, something that's lodged itself into his mind like a fishhook, that jagged, backwards barb impossible to dislodge. He's stuck with a repetition of organs and orchestral voices like he's been forced to Sunday morning church all over again. Sitting in a cramped pew, his mother and father on either side, listening to Pastor Bill talk about the Bible. It was those sermons that helped him contribute to "The Demagogue" with the band. Everyone else drew on the current feelings of politicians, watching America slide to the right in real time. Danny drew on those memories of Pastor Bill, the man saying things he'd see echoed decades later by the president.

What is this sound? Why am I thinking of this? He tries to focus on the task at hand, at setting up, unpacking, mainlining hype for the show, but he's failing. The song stuck in his head suddenly reminds Danny of this guy at college. Before he met the rest of who would later become Darrow Foroi. A guy named Matt he'd met hanging out on the lawn one day. Danny had talked with him a couple times, making conversations that never went much further than the types of movies they liked or the games they were into. Simple, fluffy, pop culture stuff. Then one day Matt said he'd been thinking about starting a club. Just some place they could hang out and talk with some other like-minded guys. A movie club or something like that.

That's how it started.

It took Danny a while to notice the kind guys who joined the club. Guys who looked like him, who talked like him, but who thought differently. Who felt the freedom to vocalize thoughts alone in a room with other familiar faces that they might never have otherwise. They said their thoughts were exploratory, that they didn't mean any harm, that they were just asking questions. Danny didn't know then that that phrase was a dog whistle.

A few years later, Danny saw guys from that club on TV, marching through the streets of Charlottesville with torches, spurned on by the voice of the Demagogue, just as people in the world of Alor would be.

It was so easy to get caught up in it, because it almost never started that way, as bigotry. At least, it didn't used to. Now things are different. Now people can wear it openly, proudly, making hate their whole identity. That's what happens when you make one of them president.

The music grows louder in his ears, the heat hotter on his body, a splinter starting to fester in his mind, to grow. That's not what splinters do, but it's what this one does. They swell, maybe, but they don't *grow*.

They don't metastasize.

Splinters don't become something different. But it is what this one does.

Splinters don't have voices.

Danny can hear it, hiding somewhere behind the music. No, not hiding. Hiding implies weakness. Fear. No, the voice is that of something strong, but waiting, biding its time. Like an alligator beneath the surface of the water. And because of that, it's distant. Danny can't hear it, though—for some reason he doesn't understand—he longs to. Even though this is the first time he's ever heard it, it brings forth memories he is familiar with: the preaching voice of Pastor Bill. Of the chant he heard on the news. The guys in Matt's club. But those things don't stir revulsion anymore.

Now they bring about a euphoria, one that that reminds him of sitting in the pews in church, only this time he feels light. He feels that goodness that had so often eluded him there.

The Festival of the Fallen Moon stands as a testament
to each and every life, love, and world that has come
before Alor. Worm walks among the celebrants, looks
into the night sky, and for the first time, feels at home.
— From Darrow Foroi's liner notes

Harley steps out into the sun when Jess's convertible pulls up. The car brakes slam, Jess intending to head up the whole drive before spotting Harley. The tires kick dirt into the air; she waves it away, wipes a couple of big flecks off her oversized sunglasses.

"How come you're not inside?"

"Parents are being weird," Harley says, bunching up her skirt in one hand and jumping over the door instead of opening it, because she's a teenager, because she can, because you're not supposed to, and especially because Jess is there, watching her.

Jess says, "You think they know?"

Harley doesn't answer because she's unprepared for what Jess is wearing—a bikini that's not metal, but is made of some glossy material that makes Harley bite her bottom lip when the sun hits it at the right angle. It looks like Jess picked a size too small—on purpose, no doubt—the way it desperately clings to her body, trying to stop her curves from escaping. She has a sarong wrapped around her waist, but it isn't covering much. There's also a collar around Jess' neck with a chain connected to it, a chain she's piled up in her lap. The whole outfit makes Harley think of *Return of the Jedi*, of dozens of different Frank Frazetta images of beautiful women standing before monsters or men with rippling muscles. Images that awoke things in her she only knew how to define as a little girl as *making her tummy feel funny*.

"What is *that*?" Harley asks, very obviously staring. It is not the first time she's stared at Jess like so, and it won't be the last.

"You like?" Jess smiles, leans back in the seat, emphasizing her nearly-nude body. She pulls on the chain coming from her collar, winding it around her wrist. She sticks her tongue out a little, makes a small choking noise followed by a mischievous smirk. Harley wonders if Jess has done this because she *knows*. Is it because she knows and she reciprocates, because she's Jess and she's a flirt, or because she just wants to show off her body, and she truly has no idea how Harley feels about her? No, Jess may *play* dumb sometimes, but she isn't actually dumb.

"It's certainly...something," Harley says, wondering if she should flirt back. How would Jess take it? Would she do anything real with it or would she continue to just...Jess? Harley is aware that what she feels is not just a physical attraction, but also a jealousy. She wishes she could be that free.

"You like it," Jess says, sitting back up, looking at her over her sunglasses so Harley can see those brown eyes. Those eyes she falls into and swims in, letting the brown consume every inch of her soul. "I see you peeking."

Harley is peeking, she can do nothing else. And she will continue to peek, as she has before. She remembers the first time like it was only moments before—this fascination with her best friend that goes beyond all her other friendships, remembers sleeping over at Jess's house in middle school and how when they changed into pajamas Harley had worn an oversized T-shirt that reached so far down her legs it might as well have been a dress, while Jess came out of the bathroom in a tank top and short shorts her butt was beginning to fall out of. Harley had never wanted to touch something more in her life.

It feels cliche, to admit that the seed for this attraction was plant-ed at a sleepover. Like the beginning of an especially cliché porn. Like Harley should have developed something better as a way to elevate the standard. But she had—and continues to have—no control over what she felt and feels, the things that are awakened in her, what she feels when she sees Jess in a bikini at the beach, or hitting the showers in gym class. That strange entangling of wanting to be *with* Jess, and wanting to *be her*.

Will she feel the same about me when I change? Harley thinks, and then when Jess cranks up the music as they're driving along the highway, it's "The Festival of the Fallen Moon" from Darrow Foroi, and Harley is struck with that gods-gifted feeling of bravery for those who are oh, so very lucky. She leans back in her seat and tugs on her skirt, pulling away the excess fabric and tossing it at her feet. She pulls open her blouse, reveals the corset underneath. Pulls the silken wrap off her head and lets her hair loose. She does it all before she can think, before she can stop herself, focusing on the music more than anything else. Much more than her own fear.

"Hell yeah!" Jess shouts. "Now we're talking!" She turns the music even louder, and they speed toward the faire, Harley's heart pumping.

MOST PEOPLE SIMPLY CALLED it the RenFest, but the full name of the festival was actually Questing Beast Renaissance Pleasure Faire, and it was clear that the pleasure had started before Harley even got there; the tradition of pregaming in the field in front of the faire was well underway.

Jess spots the rest of their crew, and squeezes her car in next to Steve's familiar red pickup. She howls with anticipation as she turns off the car, hops out into the grass. Her enthusiasm is spreading, but it hasn't fully caught Harley yet. She's smiling, trying to hide it, but it's more because she's nervous, embarrassed, timid, and afraid even in the face of this small act of rebellion.

Everyone wolf-whistles at the girls' outfits. Harley looks at the ground between her feet, but Jess makes a show of it, spinning in place and shaking the hips Harley can't help but stare at. In

Harley's experience, every friend group has one person like Jess. Usually a girl, they're someone everyone falls in love with at least once at various points of their friendship. Jess is this girl, and she knows she's this girl, and she likes it. She owns it. How Harley wishes she could channel some of that bravery.

Steve, a big guy dressed in a kilt and vest with a fox-skin draped over his shoulders, puts a plastic cup under the nozzle of a large tankard—an actual barrel—in the bed of his pickup. He pours a drink and hands it to Jess. She gives him a flirty wink and takes a sip. Steve winks back, but it's half-hearted. Everyone knows Steve is pretending to be at that specific point in their friendship, the point where he's entertaining the thought of romancing Jess. Everyone except him seems to know the direction he really leans, but no one ever pushes him.

Harley thinks a familiar thought that she's had a million times before; maybe *this* will be the day. Maybe this will be the place, the event, where she finally tells Jess how she feels. Maybe this will be where she makes a move and Jess says she feels the same. Maybe this is the beginning of everything. Harley tries to hold on to that feeling, to not let it go, because she needs it to be true. Otherwise, what, it'll just be the same circle over and over again.

But Jess is drinking, does that make it not right? Would it then make it okay if Harley starts drinking too? She doesn't know if it will, but she does anyway when Jess holds a cup out for her. Jess and the rest of their friends are used to Harley not drinking, and this moment has become a ritual between them; Jess offers, only ever once, just in case Harley has changed her mind. When Harley refuses, Jess takes the cup for herself. But this time Harley takes the cup, and Jess is flabbergasted that her hand is empty.

"You for real?" She's got that wicked smile, and Harley gazes into it for just a second too long. A second that's not long enough.

She says nothing. Instead, puts the cup to her lips and throws her head back, tilting the liquid to the back of her throat before she can second-guess herself. She's ready for the burn, and she takes it, chugs it down, only spilling a little over her cheeks, and in victory tilts the cup upside down to show everyone how empty it is. Hooting and hollering erupt around her. Someone yells "Peer pressure!" and Harley's head is swimming, regretting it already, until she teeters and Jess reaches out and grabs her by the elbow, holds her steady.

"Whoa," she breathes, so close to Harley, "that's my giiiirl." It's like a purr. Like a cat ready to wrap its tail around its mate.

Harley can feel Jess's breath on her face, and mint has never smelled so appealing.

Someone wolf whistles, and when Harley looks over, she almost jumps in place. There's something lecherous in her friends' eyes—all of them, all at once—coinciding with some out-of-place choral music coming from speakers somewhere. What's in her friends' expressions is something sinister, made that much more ominous by the presence of the music. It's only there for a second.

For such a brief moment that maybe, if Harley tries hard enough, she can convince herself she didn't see it at all. But some deep part of her brain tells her she can't do that, can't ignore it. That, in fact, she's in danger. She gets the feeling like she's surrounded by a pack of wolves, and though they don't seek flesh from her, what they want is something equally awful.

Jess doesn't seem to have noticed this change in their friends at all. She's a lightweight, or at least she acts like it, and clings to Harley, her fingers pressing into her arms, her shoulder. The way Harley wants, has wanted for so long, but not like this. Not under these circumstances.

"S'matter?" Jess slurs with actual concern for Harley. When Harley looks back to their friends, those predatory glances are gone, all of them returned to normal, drinking and chatting and not paying attention to the two of them. That music is gone too.

"Nothing," Harley says, patting Jess on the back and taking another drink. She holds onto this one, sipping mostly from her water bottle and keeping her friends in front of her until it's time to head toward the gates, to ready for the opening.

WHEN THE QUESTING BEAST Renaissance Festival opens, it's to the sound of actual trumpets. A bearded man dressed as a Middle Ages king with his silver-haired queen by his side appears on the ramparts and announces the official seasonal opening. The drawbridge lowers and period music plays, and people dressed in all manner of costume start streaming into the faire under a rain of flower petals thrown from the ramparts by court jesters. Greeters at the gates address the patrons with period dialog and displays of juggling and fencing and exotic costumes.

The enormous crowd disperses throughout the faire, heading to mead tastings or glass-blowing at the forge, or just wandering around to look at all the amazing sights, wondering at the ingenuity of this time-lost place. The majority of the fairgoers are in costume, a few in clothes that would give away the fact that they just walked in off the street in the twenty-first century, but all of them are having fun. There are a few groups continuing an eternal RenFair joke; groups in Starfleet T-shirts, a pair of old pals dressed as Doc Brown and Marty McFly wandering around looking confused and enthralled. Everyone is smiling. Everyone is laughing. Everyone is staring in wide-eyed awe.

Seeing all this, it's hard to imagine there's anything wrong with the world.

That, at least, is how Nathan Biggs feels. Maybe it's because he spearheaded the building of this place. Or because it was such a long endeavor, because he was so meticulous about its construction. Maybe it's because he can go on social media, even after wandering the faire himself, and see the happy faces of all the people who've passed through. But most likely, it's because it's something much bigger than him. Because it's something more now.

Below, somewhere in that swelling mass, are the evening's entertainment. Mr. Quest, Darrow Foroi, the Musicians of Bremen. For the bands, it's still several hours until curtain, and they're free to roam the faire as fans, experiencing everything it has to offer.

Lo is disguised, appears just as much a renaissance maiden as anyone else in the crowd. Not a rocker, not entertainment. Not stuck in an uncomfortable liminality, but feminine for today, because that's what their body is telling them. Heeled boots that prop them up and push them out, a purple skirt that swishes around their waxed legs, penis tucked, invisible. Hair extensions that drape curls down over their exposed shoulders. A white blouse and a corset pulling in their waist, pinching them in the middle.

This, the feeling of euphoria, is why they wrote "The Festival of the Fallen Moon". All these feelings of bliss channeled into song.

Women compliment their skirt and tell them their hair looks great. Even a few of the beer-slicked side-eyes from men send a thrill up their spine. Men want them because men want women and today, Lo is a woman. It's caveman logic, antiquated, and Lo knows there's a problem in there that may need to be unwound, but they don't bother dealing with that problem right now, only bask in the feeling. Everything is right with the world.

It is much easier like this, Lo thinks, to blend in. To be on one side of the line rather than straddling it, rather than enduring the questioning looks and quasi-attractedness, people constantly wondering who or what you were. Today is a day they feel like one thing, but what about tomorrow? What will they feel then?

Tomorrow can wait until tomorrow.

THERE'S NO DOUBT IN Nathan Biggs's mind that they are doing the right thing when it comes to the faire, the secret shows. There's the right thing, the moral thing, and then the legal thing. They're not often the same. They sure aren't now. Seems like they rarely ever have been, but now they're approaching truly nightmarish territory. Territory where Biggs had to make actual, concrete plans in case the state tried to take his grandkids from his daughter and her wife. That theoretical exercise of *what would you do if you were in Germany in 1939?* is playing out before him, and he's watching his neighbors turn into Nazis. Sometimes literally. He's seen the protesters whenever they're out there on the news, the men with their red shirts and black flags standing in front of health clinics or synagogues or schools. Cowards who maybe know at least on some level they should be ashamed of what they believe in because they won't even uncover their faces.

So when Burke's voice comes in over the walkie, tells him they've got a problem at the front gate, Biggs knows now's the time to put his money where his mouth is. He's prepared for something like this; the cops, protesters. Overt violence. He'd hoped it would never come to that, but he isn't naive. He knows the lengths people will go to in the name of hate.

"What is it?" Biggs asks into his walkie, pushing past the people and the stalls towards the front gates. As he moves, he hears a series of distant pops and realizes he's more on edge than he thought when he thinks, *Oh, sweet Jesus, it's gunfire.* Except he's heard gunshots before in wartime and on the target range and these sound more like fireworks. Not exactly like fireworks, though. Whatever they are, they're coming from where Burke is, from the front gates, followed by a strange, low sound, almost like a groaning.

There's a hidden entrance in the fake castle wall to his right and he slips inside, heads up to the ramparts, moving above all the people below. He can see Burke over by the entrance, looking over the edge and out into the field.

"It's... I ain't sure."

Biggs hustles, gets there, and follows the invisible line drawn by Burke's finger out into the open field. The sun's going down, but it's not the only light out there. Over the fields of parked cars, Biggs can see what looks like headlights but he knows cannot be. There are dozens of them, and they all move together, like they're following a path, a leader, someone cutting their way through the field and the cars. But there's no engine noise that comes with these lights, and they flicker like flame, aren't steady like glass. Orange, not white, vaporous, like the will-o'-the-wisps he's sometimes seen in the swamps. And with the lights, that strange sound coalesces, and Biggs hears music. It's distant, hard to decipher, but it sounds like church music. Like chanting.

Biggs has heard something like this before. From the men with the flags.

There's something awful, something evil, in the light out there in the field. Biggs can't stand to look at it anymore, can't stand the way it makes him feel. It's making him sick. He thinks he's gonna hurl, but it doesn't matter, as that the bizarre mix of light and sound that lurks before the gates comes forward, crashing against the walls of the faire, the organ music climaxing and the chanting crescendoing and the walls are blown apart, letting the light in.

HARLEY'S FRIENDS BREAK OFF into groups after a while, as they usually do during the faire, meeting for lunch or a show or bumping into one another as they try to catch a sight of the endless attractions.

Jess, thankfully, does not leave her side.

There are so many wonderful things to see, but Harley often finds herself looking back at Jess. Sword-swallowers and flame-spitters and knife-jugglers, people on stilts and merchants hawking their wares, tremendous costumes that look like they're pulled straight out of the past, turkey legs dripping with gravy.

And between all those spectacles is her best friend. The person who convinced her to do this in the first place. To be brave. Harley doesn't realize it in the moment, but she's forgotten all about the outside world. She's forgotten about her nerves coming into the faire to begin with, forgotten about how exposed and vulnerable she felt in her new outfit. Forgotten about her parents. For just a little while, the rest of the world doesn't exist, and isn't that the point?

Harley and Jess spend all day together, Jess often leading Harley around by the hand, which sends a little flutter through her heart. They go to the axe-throwing booth and Jess throws her arms around Harley and screeches when she nails a bullseye. They meet Steve and the rest of the gang for the noonday joust, listen to the faire's story of two knights competing for a princess' hand in marriage. They holler as the joust ends in a spectacular explosion of lances, one knight falling to the ground, conceding his defeat. They sit in the shade to get away from the afternoon sun, and when Jess gets sleepy she leans her head against Harley's shoulder and takes a nap.

Harley's so distracted by it all she almost forgets about Darrow Foroi and their concert, but the thought of them returns as the sun gets lower, as she hears people whispering about the secret show that's going to happen soon. Jess stirs from her shoulder, yawns, stretches, and Harley's brain is overflowing with the endorphins of the day, with the rush of the upcoming show, and decides there will never be a better moment than this, that it's all or nothing.

She turns and kisses Jess.

It's quick, soft, a middle school closed-mouth peck on the lips, Harley leaning in before quickly leaning back out, not realizing she needs to read the expression on Jess's face right after it happened. She sees the flush in Jess's cheeks, the wideness of her eyes, and knows hers must match.

Jess breathes, "Why did you do that?"

"I don't know. I... I had to." It's not a lie. It was—it *is* a need, and she doesn't know what that means, if that excuses her from anything because what if Jess doesn't want this? Harley's convinced it's going to turn bad, that what she's just done has ruined not just the day, but an entire life's worth of a friendship. She wonders why she did it, why she categorized it as a need—*So stupid so so stupid and selfish*—but then she feels the pull, and realizes the pull is not Jess's gravity, not what she feels when she's around her, but what she literally feels here, now.

It's Jess's arms, her hands, they're holding her hips, and they're pulling her closer, their pelvises touching, and then their stomachs, their chests, their lips. Their arms entwine around one another and it's finally happening, they're there and they're together.

And then there's the sound of an explosion in the distance.

Gods require sacrifices. And when Worm feels their
head swimming, feels the funny taste in their wine,
they know they have been chosen. They know they have
been betrayed.
— From Darrow Foroi's liner notes

HARLEY AND JESS STAND together for a moment, unsure if what sounded like the explosion they just heard was real, wondering if it was instead the blood pounding in their heads, the echo of their kiss. But when they listen, they hear he crowd has quieted, and when they glance around they see other worried faces looking for comfort. Everyone turns in the direction of the echoing sound. Harley and Jess peel apart from their embrace, but they do not let go of one another entirely. Jess is still holding her hand, and for that Harley is grateful.

Jess says, "That sounded like a crash," even though she knows it wasn't.

Harley says, "It sounded like an explosion," even though she somehow knows it's something much, much worse.

They wonder if whatever they just heard was a one-off, perhaps some heavy piece of machinery turning on or backfiring, one of the faire workers dropping some section of wall or attraction that still needs to be erected, a clumsy fumble. But they can hear something else in the wind, distant and low-pitched. It's organ music that everyone first seems to think is part of the show; their expressions relax, the tension in their shoulders unwinds. Some of them go back to chatting with their friends.

But beneath that music there's something else. A terrible moaning drifting toward them, the sounds of people groaning in agony.

And following in its wake, screams.

THERE'S A "WARDROBE MALFUNCTION" level of planning to Darrow Foroi's dress reveal. It isn't as severe as the infamous Janet Jackson nipple slip, instead a sort of low-rent version. There's nothing that's been specifically fabricated to come apart, but there's a degree of taping, of tucking folds into belts, tying easily-unraveling knots with string. They're wearing their dresses under most of their existing renaissance gear, and none of them really thought about the Florida sun in advance. But what's a rock concert without a little sweat and grime, a little running makeup?

Thankfully for Lo, it's still a day where a dress feels right, where they're elated by the feel of the fabric brushing against their bare legs, of the sun on their exposed shoulders, long hair tickling the back of their neck. They're not hiding their dress, not doing some big reveal once they're onstage like the boys are—it seems a little pointless when you're in a dress onstage most of the time anyway.

The one they've chosen is simpler, even, than the dress they've been wearing to wander the faire. Lo's whole look splits the rock and renfaire right down the middle; heavy rocker makeup, dark lipstick, a corset cinching them in the middle, bending their torso into an hourglass, black boots, black nail polish, purple skirt. The hem of the skirt is much shorter than they've ever worn in public. After all, they want the transphobes to look. They want them to wonder, to think they can see it if they get at just the right angle. Lo wants them to know who they are, that bigots can't shove them into a box of being one thing or the other, that there is no binary.

Lo wants to make them frothing mad.

And it's in this look that they're planning on storming the stage, starting the concert with "Godkiller" before the band even does any introductions. Those can come later. Get the crowd fired up first.

There are bigger bands in the lineup; the Musicians of Bremen, Mr. Quest, bands Darrow Foroi is meant to lead into. By the time those heavy hitters take the stage, the crowd will know full well what's going on, what all these different bands are here to do and say, and who they are here to say it to. The statement is really going to be made with Darrow Foroi, the first band onstage. Which is almost more pressure.

"What do you think the deal is with kilts?" Evan asks, holding up a kilt before him. He's not planning on wearing a kilt, but instead a floral, spaghetti-strap dress that goes down to his knees. It's on the bench in front of him. "Does a kilt count as crossdressing?"

Lo says, "Depends on who's wearing it." They know the technicalities, know they will be enforced only when those who made the rules want them to be enforced. Like transwomen who go topless in protest of being unable to change their gender on official documents still arrested for indecent exposure.

"Yeah, point," Evan says, sounding defeated, and puts the kilt back on the rack. He picks up the dress he's going to wear and starts to pull it over his head.

Across the room, Micah prods Danny, who Lo realizes has been sitting there, lost in thought, staring off into a corner of the room. Is he getting cold feet?

"You gonna get ready, man?" And then: "Hey, Danny, you alright, dude?"

A beat before something that sounds so unlike Danny, but nevertheless uses his voice. "You're gonna let him dress like that? Parade him around like he's a real woman?"

A frigid silence blankets the room.

Lo is distantly aware of Micah asking, "What did you say?" but it doesn't entirely register, because their body has snapped into fight-or-flight mode. Or at least it tries. It's stuck on the secret third option: freeze. Lo is rooted to the spot, staring at the sudden threat across the room. The whys and hows are irrelevant. The threat remains.

"Danny?" Tijo asks.

Slowly, like in a horror movie, Danny turns around in his seat. And, like in a horror movie, Lo expects to see some hideous grotesquerie of a face where Danny's should be. Those kind and gentle eyes perverted. And they are, in a way. But what looks out from Danny isn't any demonic, red-eyed stare or some hideous pus-leaking mouth, something crawling beneath his skin. It's shocking to see the intensity of his all too human hatred. It's an expression Lo has seen too many times, from loved ones and strangers alike. It's Danny in there. One hundred percent. But he's turned. Become *wrong*. Like he's lived an entire life on a different path, a bigoted, hateful path, and now that Danny from another version of the universe has come here to do the only thing men like that do.

"You dirty fucking tranny." The words stab at Lo.

Danny shoots up from his seat, across the room, right at Lo. The rest of the band are too shellshocked by this sudden and unexpected violence to react in time, and Danny has his hands around Lo's throat, hauls them up and off the bench and into the air, crushing the life out of them.

HARLEY IS MOVING BEFORE anyone else. Jess's hand is in hers and she's yanking her away from the screams while the rest of the crowd stands there and gawks. Including Jess. Harley can feel her stumble as they move, worries she's hurting her with as hard as she's pulling. Some deep, primordial sense tells her that whatever's on the other end of that music and those screams will do much worse than hurt her. It'll do something inconceivable, and she knows she has to get them both away from there.

Harley's movement activates the rest of the crowd, resets them from their stupor, and when they see one person running, then everyone is running and screaming and trying to get away. Before she knows it there's a torrent of people, a stampede of bodies shearing its way through the faire.

"What's happening?" Jess calls from over her shoulder. Her voice is distant, like she's not really in her body. "Where are we going? What are we doing?"

Harley doesn't have any answers, only knows she has to get them away, has to keep them safe. She shouts, "Just stay with me!", pulling Jess out of the crowd and uphill like she's trying to outrun a flood, and it works, most of the people following the path of least resistance, straight or downhill. At the top of the hill before them, there's a little chapel Harley knows has been used for weddings, where in past years they've had small shows on the patch of grass before it. There's a door in the side of the chapel, and that's where she heads. A structure pretending to be a full building, she knows there's nothing more than a storage closet beyond that door, but it's a hiding place, and it's all she has now because in all the running they might get trampled. Run, hide, fight. She'd had enough active shooter training in school to know what she was doing.

"The church!" she shouts, pointing, some part of her brain willing it to become an actual church. Hallowed ground, even though she doesn't believe in that. But maybe it is true, maybe the stories are real and she tries so hard to make it true, make the church a *real* safe space. For it to protect them.

On the climb, Harley only takes one look over her shoulder, back behind Jess, and she cannot put into words what she sees. She tries, but knows they won't do the sight justice; there's something gliding through the faire, above the crowd of fleeing people, draping itself over them. It looks like a mist. Or maybe it's a light. Maybe it's somehow both? Not all, but many of the people touched by the strange shimmer-like thing slow down, stop their running, and stand there as if dazed. She sees Steve, a head taller than most in the crowd, stop running and slow to a strange, transfixed sway. He and everyone else in the crowd look around, seemingly wondering where they are. Harley looks away, knowing—somehow—that looking straight at this shimmering mist is like looking at the sun; do it for too long and she's going to get hurt. Something bad's going to happen. The strange sight is accompanied by that organ music, by the sound of chanting in a language she doesn't think she, or any person, possesses the ability to understand.

She tries to flee from it, but Jess has stopped in her tracks. She too is looking over her shoulder, down at the crowd that's been swallowed by the glowing mist.

"What are you doing?" Harley pulls on her, but she's rooted to the spot, almost immovable. "Jess!" Harley gets in front of her, aware of the light, the mist, creeping its way up the hill toward them, of the music getting louder, the organs and the chanting, how she can make out specific words now. Jess's head is tilted up towards the sky, her eyes rolled back into her head, only showing whites.

"Jesus Christ, Jess!" She has no idea what to do when someone is having a seizure, if that's even what's happening to her, but she knows something worse than this is going to happen if that light catches them, and so Harley lowers her shoulder and shoves a backwards-stumbling Jess uphill towards the church as the light chases them. She looks over her shoulder, and swears the light, the fog, displays some sort of sentience, that it *turns*, having sensed them as prey, and pursues them uphill, the music getting louder as it encroaches. Harley pushes with all her strength, and Jess seems to come out of the trance, to realize they need to move, and she stumbles up the hill, stands there while Harley whips the door open. They're inside only moments before the light and the mist touch the closed door behind them, and Harley is grabbing a tarp off a shelf next to her and shoving it under the door because she doesn't know how this mist works but what if it can get under the door, what if it can get them that way but that doesn't seem to matter because the walls of the faux-church around them are shaking so hard the whole thing might collapse, and Harley knows this is no holy place.

LO STARES DOWN THE length of Danny's fuzzy arms to his face. They don't recognize him. Danny has become something different, something horrible. In those eyes, it's not Danny. They don't know if they tell themself that because they truly believe it, or because they're simply unwilling to accept that their friend could ever do them harm. Neither makes sense. Neither erases the reality of Danny's hands around their neck, of Lo's back against the wall, of the air being crushed from their throat and the spots appearing in their eyes.

Micah, Tijo, and Evan are all on Danny, pulling at his arms, trying to twist his fingers, leaping on his back. Kicking. Punching. Anything to get him to release his hold on Lo. But he's not giving up. Growling like a rabid dog as he pulls Lo closer to his face.

"You bitch," he growls, but his voice doesn't sound like him. There's something else inside it. Behind it. "Do you think you can do this?"

Lo has no idea what he means, just wants him to stop hurting them.

And then Evan pulls the gun. He jams it against Danny's temple. Danny doesn't even register it. Micah moves towards Evan, who gives him a warning look. Both he and Tijo back away. There's only Evan, Danny, Lo, the gun. Lo's beginning to lose strength, thinks they're going to pass out.

Evan says, "Danny, you get one goddamn warning!"

But Danny ignores him, growls in Lo's face as they paw futilely at his gripping fingers. There's spots in their eyes, darkness on the edge of their vision, but also something in their ears. Music? Chanting? It sounds familiar.

"Danny, put Lo down or I'm gonna fuckin' shoot you!" Evan's voice cracks, his hand shaking.

Nothing Evan says is getting through: not the voice, not fists, not even the barrel of the pistol against his temple. Can Danny hear the music too?

"Fuck!" Evan pulls the gun away from Danny's head, presses it hard into the meat of his bicep. "I'm sorry, man," and pulls the trigger.

The sound is so much louder than movies told any of Lo it would be. It is literally an explosion. A small explosion, but an explosion nonetheless, one that obliterates the music from Lo's ears, leaving nothing but a high-pitched ringing. The bullet blasts through Danny's arm, the muscle exploding like a water balloon—more blood there than any of them would have thought—and buries itself in the dressing room wall, a smoking crater.

Danny finally releases Lo, falling away with heavy grunts, and Evan pushes him even further, shoving him with his shoulder across the room.

Lo falls into Micah's arms, air seeping back into their throat, and they drink it in. Micah tells them to keep their chin up, to allow air into the passage, and somehow they hear him, understand him. Somewhere to their right, Tijo asks no one in particular, "What the fuck?" over and over again.

Across the room, Danny is still shooting daggers at Lo, only tangentially aware of Evan and the gun, or even his own wound. He seems like he's going to get up, but then Evan steps down on his ankle, points the gun right into his face. He can't even form a question, can't ask what's wrong, because how would he even know to begin?

But the thing that looks up at him isn't Danny. Lo is sure of this now. Danny's eyes aren't like that. They don't have that hate in them. But nevertheless it's there, something bright and evil, staring out from them where Danny used to be.

Each member of Darrow Foroi is frozen with indecision, wallowing in the quiet, in the moment. The only sounds are Danny's heavy, salivated breathing, and Lo's choking.

It's in that quiet that they realize there are also screams, outside.

THERE'S SOMETHING HAPPENING OUTSIDE. Something bad. They all know it, but they're too focused on the something bad that's already inside with them. Evan still stands guard over Danny, the gun steadier now and trained on his chest. Micah inspects Lo's bruised throat. Tijo stands there looking between the door and his friends, horrified at all of it, struck with indecision.

Evan says, "What do we do? We gotta call somebody."

"*Cops*?" Micah asks, meaning to make the idea sound as idiotic as it actually is.

"No," Evan says, but he doesn't follow it up with an alternative.

Lo checks their phone. They all do. Even if they figured out who to call, they weren't calling anyone. It's their phones. No service. Tijo even tries the landline attached to the wall. Nothing. Evan shoves Danny to the side and takes the phone from his pocket, just in case.

"Nope." He throws it to the floor, cursing.

"Maybe we can make a run for it," Tijo says, peering outside. "The car isn't far. It's just on the other side of the office building." Maybe a hundred yards away.

"What about him?" Micah gestures to Danny.

"Fuck him." Lo glares at him, and they're surprised by the venom in their voice. This isn't the first time someone Lo's trusted has turned against them. And, unfortunately, it probably won't be the last. But...has Danny really turned against them? Is that really Danny sitting there, or is Lo just trying to construct some narrative that wouldn't make him responsible for what he's just done? Something that would save their friend in their eyes?

Danny leans forward, growling. "You wanna be a woman so bad? Come here, I'll show you what a woman does." Those words, that voice, they aren't his. It's not just a hope, Lo knows that for sure, and yet they cannot tell exactly why they know that, what separates this voice from the Danny they knew. It's indescribable in the same way that angry music was indescribable. Something they can *feel* more than *understand*.

"Shut the fuck up!" Evan jams the barrel of the gun into Danny's cheek.

Micah says, "Tijo, what can you see outside, man? What's going on out there?"

"I don't know. It's some kind of...riot, I think."

"What do you mean?"

"The fairgoers," he says, "they're...they're all attacking each other."

Micah goes over to the door, looks out, and Lo follows him, rubbing at their throat. When they get to the door, Micah's got an arm over the doorway, clearly about to try to stop them, to tell them they don't need to see this, but Lo shoots daggers at him and he backs down. Remaining as still and quiet as possible, they peer outside. The costume warehouse is far away from the public part of the faire, half-hidden by a wall and part of a hill. Through what little gaps they have, they spy people running through the dark, fleeing like they're being chased.

Because they are.

Pursuing them are strange figures. Not quite people, but not quite the mirages Lo initially wanted to describe them as. They're something in between. Like people witnessed through a heat shimmer, their outlines wriggling and stuttering, blurring and congealing randomly. It hurts Lo's head to look at them, and whenever they do, they can hear that strange organ music repeating in their head, that chanting bouncing around inside their skull. Despite the hurt of looking at them, they notice something.

"Not all of them are attacking each other."

"What do you mean?" Micah asks.

Lo explains to them the pattern they see, the normal-looking people fleeing those blurred figures.

"Shit, you're right," Micah says.

Lo rubs their throat again. They turn away from the door and look at Danny. His rage has subsided somewhat, and he at least no longer looks like he's going to try and test Evan's skill with the gun, seems content to sit and hold his arm and glare at each person in the room in turn.

"Hey," Lo calls him and Danny turns. "What is this?" They don't know what they're doing, don't know if Danny has any kind of information on what's happening outside. But it seems like a coordinated attack, and it's hard to believe Danny's sudden and violent outburst happening at the exact same time has nothing to do with it. He doesn't seem to be like the attackers outside, but neither is he entirely himself. "Answer me, Danny."

"Fuck you, faggot. It puts a dress on and thinks it's a woman."

Hurtful words. Words Lo has heard before. They try to not let it show on their face, hold up a hand to stop the rest of the band's protestations.

"I said answer me, Danny. What's happening outside?"

"I'm not talking to you."

"Fine," Lo says. They look at everyone else. "Then we tie him up and leave his ass here."

Micah already has a long, leather belt off the wall. "I'm cool with that."

THERE'S BARELY ENOUGH ROOM for both Harley and Jess in the little closet in the side of the church, but at least it's finally stopped shaking, whatever that was outside finally leaving them alone. Harley doesn't know if it's still out there, has no intention of opening the door, of checking outside to find out. Maybe she and Jess can stay in there until it's all over. The cramped space feels more like a confessional than a storage closet. Apt for the day, Harley thinks, and then chuckles. She's already laughing. She doesn't know if that's a sign that she's maintaining some sort of normalcy, some gallows humor in the face of this insanity, or if she's succumbed to the insanity already.

She turns to Jess, can barely see her face in the dark, but when she looks close she can see her eyes, at least see the irises now, even if her eyelids are drooping. She looks drunk, close to passing out. Harley grabs her by the face.

"Jess, don't go to sleep. Hey, listen to me! Don't go to sleep." Aren't you supposed to stop people from sleeping if they have a concussion? Or shock? Or something?

"What's going on?" Jess's speech is dreamy, her words slurred. She sounds high, almost like she's enjoying it.

"I don't know," Harley whispers back. She doesn't even know how to begin to explain what happened. Is it some sort of chemical on the wind, like a spill or some natural gas? Is it an attack? Who would do something like this? "Something's happening outside. Something bad." That's all she says. All she knows. She wishes she could put any of the pieces together, but they all feel like they come from entirely different puzzles, their corners not matching up. All she can do is sit there with Jess and hope that whatever's outside goes away if it hasn't already.

Harley can hear people, what sounds like a group, milling about. If people are out there, does that mean the mist is gone? Or are they somehow part of it? Harley tries to listen closer, can hear what sounds like, but they're too far away for her to make out any words. Their speech sounds rhythmic, like a song, and behind them is layered that strange organ music. Harley doesn't dare even crack the door, doesn't trust what she hears out there. She thinks about Steve, about all the other people who were caught in that strange fog. What happened to them? They don't seem to be shouting anymore. But what does that lyrical conversation mean? Are they the ones talking?

"We'll stay here for a while," Harley whispers, just as much to herself as Jess. "They're all outside. We'll stay here until they go away." Harley looks down at the ground, at her legs, and a knife of guilt cuts through her chest. She tells herself the two things aren't related, this incident and the way she dressed, how she came to the faire. But her mind has already connected them, already told her it's all her fault, as impossible as that is.

"So…we're trapped in here?" Jess slurs from behind her.

"Yes." Harley says, trying to drive those guilty thoughts from her mind. Correlation doesn't always equal causation. How on earth could Harley have caused this? That's what she asks herself, but her mind tells herself it doesn't matter how. That it happened. That's all that matters.

"Hmm…" Jess purrs from the dark. "Perfect." But that voice suddenly doesn't sound like Jess anymore. Not at all, but something else layered inside her voice. Slowly, Harley turns away from the door and looks at her. Jess's eyes have become lucid again, but what's behind them isn't her. It can't be her, because Jess would never look at her like that, with that wicked grin on her face.

Like Harley was prey.

"Jessica?" Harley's petrified at the quiver in her own voice, realizes she's crawling away from Jess.

Jess quickly sits up, pulls her legs under her, stretches her arms out before her, moving into a crouch. Then all fours, balanced on her toes, the whole time looking at Harley, the whole time smiling, showing her teeth.

"Oh, Harley," she coos, tilting her head to the side, a cat examining a trapped bird, "this is what you wanted. You and me alone in the dark. No friends around, no prying eyes."

Harley realizes she's backed away as far as she can go, is up against the door to the outside, only a couple feet of space between her and Jess. Or whatever this thing is. She kicks her feet out in a futile attempt to defend herself, but Jess bats them away.

"Just think of it as Seven Minutes in Heaven." Jess's words snake from her, smooth and supple and deadly. She grabs Harley's ankles and sits on her feet, pinning them down, begins crawling her way up Harley's body. "You've finally got it. Got *me*. Now you're telling me it's not what you want?" She shimmies up Harley's legs, Harley helpless to do anything about it except look into Jess's eyes as she comes closer, grabs her wrists, holds her down. So close, she can see Jess's eyes so clearly. She was wrong before. This is Jess. Not something piloting her. Not something possessing her. This is her friend, but some deep part of her brought to the surface. Brought by what, she doesn't know, but brought up just the same. Brought to the surface and amplified. She sits on Harley's lap, and some part of Harley is excited by this. She has wanted this, *wants* this, but not like this. This isn't how it's supposed to happen.

"Now, why don't you pucker up," Jess says. She opens her mouth, but it's wrong. Her jaw unhinges like a snake's with a *crack-ack-ack* of bones, her cheeks stretching, tongue long and slithering, lapping Harley's cheek. "And give me another kiss."

How does Worm stand before a god? The exact same way they would before anything else. They stand among the bowed, the humbled, the frightened. Knowing they'll be struck down. Knowing they'll be seen standing.

– From Darrow Foroi's liner notes

HARLEY TILTS BACKWARD, JESS'S too-wide mouth going for her neck. Is it a bite she's looking for, or a kiss? Harley doesn't know which one is worse.

The door falls away from behind her, and they're rolling now, tumbling downhill and away from the closet-church. They roll together, sticks and rocks and roots biting into Harley's skin. They crash into something and she feels Jess tumble away from her, grateful for the momentary reprieve, even for the pain that caused it, shocking her back to action.

Trying to pull herself to her feet, Harley is aware of the faraway sounds of screaming and fighting, of that strange music drifting on the air, but they mean nothing to her in her immediate danger. She keeps her eyes on Jess, who's rolled to the other side of a picnic table—what they must have hit—and is standing up, her back to Harley. There are cuts and scrapes on her as well, and Harley is ashamed that her mind still goes to attraction, still traces the curves of Jess's legs and her hips and the idea of wanting and wanting to possess, at such a moment.

"Jess, stop this and talk to me, okay? What the hell's going on?"

Jess turns, and there's still that manic look on her face, that terrible hunger in her eyes, and her mouth is still too big, like her jaw's been dislocated. Her tongue dangles from it like a cartoon snake's, tasting the air. Tasting Harley.

"What's going on is I want you," Jess growls, putting one foot up onto the picnic table bench like she's about to crawl over it to get to her. But she stops, merely eyeing her prey. She tilts her head to the side, frowning. "I thought you wanted me too." She makes a pouting noise.

"I..." What could she say? "I did. I *do*. But this...this isn't you."

"Of course it is," Jess says, now wearing a smile. "We may have heard the music, but we're all still ourselves."

"Music?"

"Yes, can't you hear it?" Jess says as if it's the most obvious thing in the world. She closes her eyes and tilts her head back, privy to something Harley cannot hear. Jess twirls in place like she has earbuds in, like the music is playing just for her. "It's beautiful," she says, "It can't put something in us that wasn't already there."

Jess opens her eyes. Looks at Harley. Smiles with a mouth that's too wide, filled with too many teeth. She looks... Is Jess more muscular than she was before, even a moment ago? Without so much of her clothes, Harley can see how vascular Jess looks, veins popping out under her skin, muscles bulging. Jess was never this defined. And Harley ought to know.

"Open your ears, honey, and I'll show you."

Harley can feel the music growing louder, but she claps her hands over her ears, unsure if that will do anything. She's not even sure what she's trying to protect herself from.

Jess shakes her head and waggles her finger, making a *tsk-tsk-tsk* noise. "You don't wanna listen? Then I'll make you." She lunges for her, leaps right across the table, but two shapes are suddenly on her, grabbing her.

Harley's parents.

They look strange, like Harley's looking at them through mist, or frosted glass, obscured in some way she doesn't understand. They grab Jess under the arms, haul her up and away from Harley, but they don't stop, lifting her into the air over their heads, heaving her up not with an impossible strength, but like Jess is being levitated. There's no expression on either of her parents' faces. They look nonplussed by the whole thing, as if they're doing any old evening chore, something they've done a thousand times before and will do a thousand times again.

But there is something in Jess's face as she's lifted up and away, held aloft by invisible strings as the music swells around them.

Fear.

"No, not me! Why me?" Jess shouts as she's held up between Harley's parents, feet kicking above the ground. Her parents hold

Jess between them, her father at the head, her mother at the legs, pulling her taut until they're not even holding her anymore, until Jess is levitating between the two of them, kicking and fighting against the invisible force that holds her aloft.

Harley's mother says, "You filled our daughter's head with dirty little thoughts. You'd better stay away from her!"

"Mom, Dad, no, wait!"

But there's a triumphant bellow of organ music that drowns out Harley's words, something so loud it sounds like it's right next to her. She can actually see the sound waves raking across the scene, waving their way through the trees around them and the leaves on the ground, through her parents' clothes and hair, rippling through Jess's exposed skin.

The sound pulls Jessica apart.

It isn't so much a killing as it is an *unmaking*. Harley's parents and the music, they all work together to reduce Jess to nothing, but in a way she did not know was physically possible. The pitch of Jess's screams increase as the music rises, and she's shredded to pieces by the pull of her parents and the force of the music turned physical. It rips skin and shreds muscle, boils blood and snaps bone. It looks like gravity has decided to stop working on Jess, the terrible chunks of her refusing to fall, before the music rises again and they're reduced to dust. Jess is *destroyed*, atomized, and some part of Harley understands that this is what the music wants; to obliterate its enemies, wipe them from the face of the earth, leave no trace they were ever there.

Harley knows she can't fight anymore, her limbs exhausted, shaking, wet noodles, and all she can do is flop to the ground, staring at the place in the air where Jess disappeared.

"It's okay, honey." Her mother looms over her. "That bad girl won't be able to fill your head with nasty little thoughts anymore."

THEY HOG-TIE DANNY. PUT a belt around his mouth and cinch it tight. Truss him up and leave him in the middle of the room. Everything looks like it'll hold, but it doesn't matter; even if he gets out, they'll be long gone. They need to get away, they've decided, their only plan. Whoever these rioters are, they'll find Darrow Foroi's hiding spot eventually. And they all agreed long before they ever arrived in Florida that they couldn't count on any authorities to save them.

Get to the other side of the admin building. Micah will drive. Evan will take shotgun and Tijo and Lo will be in the back, left and right. High-tail it out of there, trench the field if they have to. Whatever comes next is whatever comes next. They need to figure out a way out of the immediate danger. Run, hide, fight. They all went to public schools. They know their shooter training. Away from what's right on the other side of the door. All that matters right now is surviving. Because it won't be long until someone figures out where they are. *Who* they are. Lo tries not to think about how they might be the reason this is all happening, tries to box those fears, but plenty leak through.

"Ready?" Micah's hand's on the door. Evan's ready to provide cover, to point the pistol at any aggressors—six bullets again, after replacing the one he put through Danny's arm. Everyone knows if it comes to it, he'll fire. They see it in his eyes; he's no longer shaky and uncertain, he's controlled, focused, channelling something frightening inside him.

One by one, they all nod. Micah says, "We don't stop, don't fight unless they stop us. Unless there's no other choice."

And then before they can talk themselves out of it, Lo reaches forward and pushes the door open, stepping out of the building first.

The very air feels different outside. Hot, but not normal Florida-hot. Hot like there's a fire somewhere nearby. Like it's coming closer, the heat felt directly on their skin. Lo creeps through the grass. They can hear screams from all around the faire, people running, fighting in the distance, and that same music and chanting underneath. Lo tries their best to ignore it, to not think about how the sounds remind them of the riots on the news, neo-Nazis plowing cars through protestors, clashing in the street with innocent drag queens, people caught in the melee. They hurry with the rest of Darrow Foroi around the admin building to where all the participant cars are parked.

And they all immediately freeze in their tracks.

There's a huge crowd of...*something* around the cars, not people...or are they? It's hard to look straight at the crowd, but Lo tries, fighting against the sensory overload of the growing organ music and the blistering looking-directly-into-the-sun looks of these strange shapes. Looking at them, Lo understands. This isn't just a riot. These aren't people, whatever they are, here to do so much worse than random carnage. The figures look like they're covered in some sort of heat shimmer, a distortion keeping Lo from properly seeing them. Vague approximations of color, of features, like their mind can only understand so much of these bizarre entities. They move in a strange, choppy way, fast and then slow, speeding up and slowing down like they have random frames taken out of their ethereal animation, their own personal records skipping aimlessly. All the while that organ music accompanies them.

One large figure looks like he's giving orders to the others, pointing, seemingly telling them what to do, but his words are garbled, lyrics spit and chopped into a language Lo can't understand, like a record spinning backwards. This figure—something other than a *hu*man—looks like some barbarian warlord of yore; a kilt, thick beard, and the pelt of some large, orange animal draped over his shoulders. He's even carrying an enormous two-headed axe in one hand that looks like it's plucked right from the faire's forge. He directs the rest of the figures, and Lo watches as they sabotage cars, puncture tires and destroy engines.

Darrow Foroi's van rests on its side. All four tires of Micah's car are punctured. Every window's shattered, and both hoods are open the guts of the engines spewed out across the field.

Micah's fist is in a halt gesture. Everyone freezes, unsure of their next step. They're all still when the music rises, swelling as if the universe directs the score of their lives. The music rises. The mob turns. The music seems to turn right alongside them, pushing its way over the band, smothering them, holding them in place.

The figure in the kilt points its axe right at Darrow Foroi.

"Run!" Evan shouts, but he doesn't heed his own advice. He lifts the pistol as the mob surges forward, and Lo wants to stay, tries to help, but Micah has them by the back of their dress, is pulling them, and Tijo is behind them both, spurring them forward. But Evan is firing, moving backward, but not fast enough.

The wave of figures descends upon him. Evan fires at random into their ranks, pulls the trigger again and again and again even as the mob swallows him, and he disappears into that strange swirl.

HARLEY'S PARENTS DRAG HER through the dirt. She has no fight left in her, doesn't know what she's supposed to do or where she's supposed to go even if she did.

They drag her past the jousting pit. There are more of the blurred attackers milling about, but there's an order to most of them now. They've captured fairgoers, rounded them into a small group, standing guard over them. There's someone...some*thing*...a presence in the king's chair in the stands above the pit. It looks like a more intense version of that heat shimmer. Or at least that's Harley's first impression—*blood and bones*—because she cannot look at it for any longer than a couple moments. Some invisible force presses down on her brain, projecting terrible images—*fields of bodies, medieval warfare*—and worse thoughts—*swords, axes, spears piercing armor, cracking bone*—into her head, and she has to look away.

The door in the facade under the balcony opens, and a figure strides out into the sand. It's an enormous shape on horseback, its image warping and wriggling with the same shimmer as the rest. It's some perversion of a knight, a huge shape head-to-toe in plate armor, with a halberd dragging across the ground in the sand behind its steed. The shutter on the helmet is closed, covering the knight's face. Instead of the black Harley expected, the figure's armor is white, so immaculately white it's as if blemishes have been forbidden from touching it.

One of the attackers who Harley recognizes as a bizarrely blurred, harried Steve—the kilt, the pelt, unmistakable—drags a fairgoer before the knight, and the enormous figure descends from its horse, lifts the halberd, swings it down. It's all so fast, efficient, so quick she hasn't realized what happened, the opposite of the theatricality the moment seemed to have demanded. Almost as if the figure is bored with the whole affair. It takes Harley a moment to realize they've decapitated the hostage. That Steve, her friend, has helped in this. Something has happened to him; whatever happened to Jess, to her parents.

Harley throws up, and the things her parents have become—or maybe the things that have been unleashed from her parents—don't stop, or even bother to turn, just drag her through her own sick. They carry her away from the jousting pit, through the faire, and when Harley finds the strength to lift her head again, she wishes she hadn't.

Because they're at the stockades.

And they're full of people.

Captured fairgoers held by their necks and wrists, some screaming, but most now resigned to their fate, exhausted, lolling under their bonds. The bizarre attackers hurry about the area, building more stockades, clapping boards and nails together and filling them with fairgoers as soon as they're finished.

"Another!" one of them calls, and their voice is strange, like they're in a musical, and it's intent on hitting its note. It might sound pretty were it not for the situation. The shape approaches Harley's parents, and they jostle her indicating her. "That one," the shimmered figure says, pointing to a stockade.

Harley wants to fight, knows she should, but she doesn't have anything left. So she, like so many of the others, accepts her fate as her parents toss her into a stockade and lock her in.

LO'S NEVER RUN THIS hard in their entire life. They don't know how much they have left in them. They're given power by Micah and Tijo by their side, but they don't know for how much longer they can go.

And without Evan.

Or Danny.

They can't think about that. There's only the running.

"Keep moving!" Tijo shouts, pushing them from behind, but they have no idea where they're going. They only know through, only know to try to get to the other side of the very real carnage they can see before their eyes.

The fairgrounds have become a literal battlefield. Like something out of *The Lord of the Rings*. There's carnage everywhere; shopfronts on fire, trenches blasted into the grass, the decorated edifice at the front of the faire blown to smithereens as if hit by repeated cannonfire. Smoke clogs the air and trees are split as if by lightning, splintered ends sticking out and smoldering. Screams and the sounds of fighting, of armies crashing together, echo on the wind along with that organ music and the accompanying chanting.

And then there are the bodies.

Scattered all around are the corpses of fairgoers. Many of them look as if they were killed on such an ancient battlefield; struck down by sword or axe or arrow. Those still alive are fighting back against these strange, shimmering attackers who come at them with fists and sticks and in a few cases weapons pilfered from stalls. In some cases they fairgoers are holding their own, fighting with similarly improvised weapons—mops and brooms and chairs—shielding themselves with barricades made out of picnic tables or hiding within stalls. There are a few scattered gunshots, despite firearms not being allowed on the fairgrounds.

Seeing that sight, the fairgoers still fighting, Lo's had enough. Enough of running.

Their feet alter their path without their permission. They're still running, but now it's with a direction, to something and not from it. They jump over a small bench and under the gazebo to the forge, its lingering fire a warm invitation, and snatch a spear off a rack. She thinks of Worm, of their spear—the weapon of the commoner, not a trained warrior—and they feel something in their veins. Something charging them up, powering them, giving them a second wind.

One of the stuttering, shifting attackers has caught up with them as they slowed to retrieve the spear, and Lo thrusts the weapon forward. It isn't sharpened, but it's still a point of metal at the end of a pole. Physics puts all the force into the tip of the blunt blade, and it pierces the attacker's stomach. There's a crumpling noise from somewhere within, and the entity falls to the ground, its outline still twitching and writhing.

Lo hurries to catch up with Micah and Tijo, who have picked up swords from the forge, and are swinging at attackers as they move, just like Lo. All around them, pockets of resistance cheer and rally as they watch attackers fall, pushing back against their own aggressors. Lo swears they can hear that organ music quiet down, that accompanying chanting settle, as if it knows the fair-goers are resisting it. Lo doesn't know where they're going or why, just picks a direction and move, swinging the spear with all their strength, lancing attackers, picking up additional survivors as the band moves.

HARLEY DRIFTS IN AND out of consciousness in the stockades. She prefers the unconscious moments, because they mean she doesn't have to be cognizant of the horror the world has become.

The sounds of screams all around her.

The smell of smoke and fire.

Burning shops and trees and things she doesn't want to—*can't*—think about.

The sight of the other people in the stockades, of the bodies, of those...*things* that did this. The unconscious moments mean she doesn't have to think about Jess's horrible mouth or her parents or watching her friend be unmade. But at some point the ache in her limbs becomes too much to bear, even through being unconscious. She is forced to hunch there and see it all, smell it all, think it all. Somewhere in the delirium she hears the unmistakable sounds of gunshots. A bunch in a row—she doesn't know how many—and then just as quickly, they go silent.

She lowers her head, the tiny hope of freedom snuffed.

Drifts in an out.

She doesn't know how long it is.

She hears another scuffle in the distance and expects it to go away just as fast as the others. But it doesn't. The sounds grow louder, a chorus of voices that, for once, aren't that archaic chanting but the violent sounds of a riot.

Of resistance.

Harley opens her eyes, tries her best to adjust herself to a more comfortable position in the stockade. She can't turn her head much, but she can tell something is happening to her left. She hears the sounds of fighting, sees the blurred attackers leaving the area to investigate, to fight back. People are screaming, shouting *there*, shouting *the stockades!* and part of Harley doesn't want that hope, doesn't want to think things can go right, because how can they after this? Still, she turns and allows herself to look, to hope, and she is rewarded for it.

Charging into the stockade area are three shapes, shapes she'd recognize anywhere; a tall, dark man with braids dangling down his back, a bald, muscular, tattooed man, and a third, ambiguous shape in the center, one swinging a spear at anything in their way.

Darrow Foroi.

DARROW FOROI RUNS UP the hill in the direction of the stockades, surviving fairgoers charging with them, rallied, fighting back against the shimmering invaders. There are people held captive in the stockades at the top of the hill, slumped over like medieval prisoners.

"We gotta get 'em out!" Lo shouts, still no idea where this sudden surge of bravery is coming from, but using it nonetheless. Maybe it's the spear, maybe it's their friends, maybe it's thinking about Worm and all the reasons for the album, the band, the music at all, or maybe it's all the fear and anxiety finally—*finally*—turning outward instead of in on themself. They charge up the hill as a group of the entities charge down to meet them. Lo lowers their shoulder, flips an attacker over their back, and keeps moving towards the prisoners. They know not to fight, not for any longer than they can afford. They have no idea who or what these things are, or of what they're capable.

The prisoners see their rescue coming, and Lo can hear them cheer, see them animate, a renewed thrashing against their bonds.

The attackers brace against the resisting fairgoers, but the high ground isn't enough to stop the wave. Lo sees Micah wield his sword like a baseball bat with powerful overhand swings, Tijo swinging his own with wild vigor, and together they push into the stockades. Lo shoves the blade of her spear between the locks and the wood, popping them free with the leverage of the long shaft. One big fairgoer has a claw hammer he uses to pry the locks out. The freed prisoners cheer and rally themselves into the fight, picking up whatever is nearby, some attacking the shimmering entities with their bare hands.

Lo frees a young blond girl in a purple skirt and blouse, dirtied and bloodied from white to brown, and then, momentarily distracted, looks up through the canopy and to the night sky. It sounds like thunder, but there isn't supposed to be any rain.

"Behind you!" the girl screams, grabbing Lo and yanking them out of the way as that sound of thunder comes blasting into the scene. Lo can feel it all around them, a change in the air pressure like something powerful forcing its way into the world, demanding everything else make room for it. The sound coalesces into something familiar, and as Lo hits the ground they realize it isn't thunder, but hooves. They look up.

A white knight on horseback.

He cuts a wide path through the fighting, parting fairgoer and attacker alike. Lo watches in horror as a fairgoer falls beneath the horse's hooves, crushed into paste and ground into the dirt, their screams drowned by the thunderous hoofbeats and the swell of the ethereal orchestral music.

Lo looks down at the blond girl under them, who stares back up with a mixture of expressions, of which awe is a strangely large proportion. Lo's seen that look before; the girl's a fan. They can't even imagine what a strange set of circumstances this must be for her. "Thanks, kid." Lo stands and offers a hand, pulls the girl to her feet. "Stay with me, okay?"

The girl nods.

All around them, now that everyone has registered the knight's presence, the fighting starts to resume. Fairgoer and attacker crash into one another again. Stockade locks are broken. The ethereal chanting begins anew. Bodies and weapons slam together. Screams bounce off the walls of the faire, screech up to the canopy.

Across the battlefield, the knight in white armor pivots to glare at Lo. The horse stomps at the ground, digging furrows in the dirt. The knight adjusts his halberd. Tijo charges the knight, jumping out of the crowd, but the knight retaliates with a whip from the base of his halberd, catching Tijo across the side of the head. He disappears back into the crowd.

It's staring across the field at the knight when, Lo realizes they're completely out of their element. They trust themself in a fight, but this isn't that—no parking lot scuffle or mosh pit or drunken bar brawl. This is a *war* of a kind they are unfamiliar with, and whatever this thing is, the music, the knight, the entities around them, they all have far more experience than anyone else here.

The knight spurs the horse forward, and it blows through the crowd just as indiscriminately the second time, knocking down anything in its path. Lo keeps the girl behind them and puts the stockade between them and the knight, gives them enough breathing room where he doesn't even take an exploratory swing.

Not at them, at least.

He shoots past them and Lo watches as his halberd comes down into the back of a fairgoer in a Starfleet T-shirt. At least it isn't red. Well, not at first. The knight kicks out with his foot, peeling the fairgoer off his halberd as he comes around for another charge.

"This is insane," Lo mumbles. "We can't win this." They look around and see everyone has been freed from the stockades. "Micah!" they shout.

They can't see where the response comes from, but hear "Lo!"

"We've got to run! Everybody!" they shout as loud as they can. "Get out of here!" Lo hears the blond girl tell them to watch out, but it's too late. Something slams into their back, knocking them to the ground, the spear out of their hand. They tumble halfway down the hill, coming to a stop only when they slam into a tree.

When air starts to seep back into their lungs, Lo looks up and sees what hit them—the big man in the kilt, the one from the crowd that swallowed Evan.

He towers over Lo, and they can see the terrifying bulge of an erection under his kilt and a look of confusion in his ever-shifting face. Lo recognizes that look, has seen it on the faces of dozens of men who thought they were owed some sort of explanation on their existence. The confusion of whether or not the men were attracted to Lo, and whether or not they wanted to kill them for it.

And then the girl in the purple skirt is between them. Her arms thrown out, she looks up into the big man's face.

"Steve. It's me. I know you're in there, okay? Don't do this."

But the big man swats her aside like she's no more than a sapling. "Harlot," he growls in a voice that sounds too musical, too light for its intention, like it's trying to sing along to match the surrounding music. "And you," he says, turning his attention to Lo. He reaches down, grabs them by the throat, and with an impossible strength hauls them one-handed up and off their feet. "Little boys don't play dress-up."

Lo has had more than enough of men grabbing them.

They jam their thumb into the man's eye and he howls in pain. They crank their foot back and ram their boot right into his crotch. They feel something give way under their kick, and the kilted man drops them, hands going between his legs. Lo lands in a crouch, looks up.

Just in time to see a jagged shape burst out of his chest.

A thick glob of blood splatters Lo's face as they backpedal, losing their balance on the hill. They fall to their back, but don't roll, can only stare up as the attacker is lifted into the air atop the tip of the knight's halberd. The knight looks up at the kilted man, who's gone limp, and Lo doesn't know how, but they can feel a look of disgust on the knight's face through the plated armor.

A few feet away, the blonde girl looks up at the display, horrified in such a way that confirms to Lo that this is personal, that she has a stake in this beyond it simply being a horror before her eyes. She'd called him Steve. He was her friend. He was a Danny.

The knight flicks his halberd, tossing the kilted man as if he weighs nothing. He soars over the melee, the battle pausing for a moment as he flies. Slams against a tree. Hits the ground. The knight turns their horse, halberd still pointed at the kilted man as he struggles to lift himself to his feet.

"You," the knight bellows, the music rising with his voice. "You are tainted." As he moves, the rest of the attackers seem to give up on the fairgoers, push them away, but don't go in for the kill. Their attention is instead on the knight, who turns his halberd and calls out several additional attackers with severe points.

"All...of...you," he growls, enunciating as he picks out new targets, "*traitors.*"

And then the attackers descend upon their own brethren, the battle with the fairgoers forgotten in an instant. Lo sees limbs torn from bodies, teeth finding skin. When they scream, it's in that harsh, choral music.

"Lo!"

Micah and Tijo rush to their side, grabbing them, and then they're running along with the other fairgoers, escaping while they have the chance.

THEY HAVE TO STOP. Lo can't go on anymore. Something in their back hurts, and though Micah offers to carry them instead of hovering at their side like he is, they know it won't help. They need to stop. The retreat around them is chaotic, people running in every direction while the attackers are distracted. Some fairgoers take off into the swamp, others into the woods. Plenty run toward the entrance, to keep running under the power of their own feet, when they find what happened to their cars.

But Lo can't run that far. Getting thrown by the knight, rolling down the hill, hitting the tree that wounded them. They don't know how badly, don't want to know, just know they need to stop.

"In here." Tijo shoulders open the door to a tavern, and they head inside. The blond girl is still with them. Lo realizes she's on their other side, holding them up. Tijo slams the door shut behind them when they're all safe inside and Lo immediately collapses to the floor. Micah and Tijo throw everything they can up as a barricade, while the girl crouches down, her hands hovering over Lo, not quite sure what to do.

"You alright?" Lo asks.

"Wha...*me*?"

"Yeah, you." Lo looks at the rashes and scrapes on the girls wrists and neck where she was held up in the stockade. There's leaves in her hair and she's got a shiner and busted lip from where the guy in the kilt hit her.

"Yeah, I...I'm fine."

Lo believes her, for now. It's the same *fine* as Lo; clearly very not, but the only time to deal with it will be if they actually live through this. "What's your name, kid?" Lo breathes.

"Harley," the girl says. "She/her."

"Heh," Lo huffs, the pain in their back throbbing, but not screaming. "Guess you know who we are."

"Yeah." Harley smiles, and then seems to realize how strange it must look on her face, so she stops. "Not exactly how I thought meeting my favorite band was gonna go."

Lo can't help smiling. "Aw." They squeeze Harley's hand. To Micah and Tijo they say, "We're her favorite." Then: "You see any water or anything around here, Harley?"

She looks up behind the bar. "Yeah, hold on." She goes off, and Lo looks at the front door, to Micah and Tijo's barricade. They're looking at one another, remaining silent.

"I can't hear anything," Micah whispers, and Tijo shakes his head in acknowledgment. "You think the other people got away?"

Tijo says, "I hope so," but it's clear he has no clue.

Harley returns to Lo with a room-temperature water bottle, and then passes others to Micah and Tijo.

"Thanks," Micah says, ripping the cap off and downing half of it, pouring the other half over his head. "I think we're okay for now." He says it like he's trying to convince himself as well, leans up against the wall next to the door. "I think everyone else probably got away when those things all turned on one another."

"What even are they?" Harley asks. "They're people, but they're... Something's...something's wrong with them."

Tijo says it first. "Danny."

Lo nods. "He called me a fucking tranny." They realize they're crying silently and wipe at their face.

"That *wasn't* Danny," Micah says, though to Lo it sounds like he's trying to convince himself as much as everyone else. "Not our Danny."

Lo glares across the room at him. "You didn't look into his eyes. That was Danny in there, Micah. But there was... It was like there was something else in there with him too."

"What the hell does that mean?" Tijo asks.

Harley says, "I could see it in Jess too. My friend, I mean. She changed, like those other people. And my..." Her voice hitches, like she doesn't want to say what's coming next. When she finally does, she can only say so much before her voice cuts off, refusing to work. "My parents too. They were in there, but it was like they'd been twisted." Harley claps a hand over her mouth.

"But *how*?" Micah asks, desperate to find some logic. "Did somebody put PCP in the water or something?"

Lo knows. "It's the music."

They're all silent. They can hear it outside the walls. Distant. Calling. Growing stronger.

Harley gasps. "I've heard it every time something happened." Her eyes widen. "My parents were listening to it before I left. I thought there was something wrong with their record. The next time they were..." She doesn't finish, doesn't need to. The evidence of her unspoken words is all around them, in the carnage and obliterated bodies.

"The music," Tijo says, encouraging elaboration.

"The music," Lo says again, sure of it now, putting the pieces together, their brain moving faster than their mouth. "The music is doing this. The motel." They look at Micah and Tijo, and know they remember.

"But why make them kill each other?" Micah asks.

"I...I think I know," Harley says. After a deep breath, she tells them about her friend Jess and how she became one of those things, about her parents and how they tore Jess to shreds. "I think they knew," she says. "My parents. They knew about Jess and me. We...well, we kissed."

"So, the guy in the kilt..." Lo leads, remembering the towering figure and his hulking erection, the way the knight turned on him.

"My friend Steve. Everyone knows he's...*knew*, I guess. Everyone knew he was...well, he wasn't straight."

The answer snaps into place in Lo's mind. "Jesus Christ." They put their head in their hands.

"What?" Micah asks.

"They're fucking eradicating us."

"What...what do you..."

They explain to them about the kilt man's erection, about Harley's parents, about the things Danny called them all when he turned, the pattern of how those people attacked the fairgoers. It's impossible to ignore. It's their worst nightmare, exactly what they feared when they came to a hostile state. And now they're in a tiny kingdom in the middle of the country fallen to a fascist power.

"No," Tijo says, shaking his head. His voice is distant, like at the bottom of a well. "No, no, that's crazy. That's not..." He trails off, the logic overpowering him. He leans against the wall, flops harshly down to the floor, his legs giving out on him. He mutters to himself, too low for anyone to hear. After a moment he shakes his head, clearing his thoughts. "So, what do we do? We've got to get out of here, right? Tell somebody?"

Micah says, "It sounds insane to say, but I think we can all probably agree this is a situation that actually necessitates cops."

Tijo says, "I agree."

Lo says, "Yeah, maybe."

The room hushes, looks at Lo. They look up at Micah and Tijo.

"*Maybe*?" Tijo asks. "You want to go out there and fight?"

"I didn't say fight. Besides, how do we know cops won't be affected if they come here? We could just be calling more of these...bad guys, whatever, over to us. And these ones would have guns."

"Then what's your plan?" Tijo asks. "I'm with Micah on this one. We should run. We don't need to be brave."

Micah agrees, and together they keep talking, but Lo isn't paying attention. They're hearing them, but they're not listening, caught on one word in particular. *Brave*. Bravery. Is that what Lo felt every time they went outside looking like something other than how they were born? Is bravery what they feel now, that fire in their chest, the adrenaline still in their veins? Not really. Not at all.

It's anger.

They're tired of being brave. Tired of being *strong*. Tired of having to fight just to exist. Just to justify their own existence.

And now they're fucking *angry*, and a sudden image of Worm standing before the Dawn Queen pops into their head. There's a reason they wrote these songs, a reason they spent so much time poring over every lyric, every note. A reason it all had to be right.

"Lo, are you listening to me?"

Lo looks at Micah. "We do what we came here to do."

And then Lo lays out a plan that sounds insane on its face but unmistakable in its feeling.

"They'll kill us," Harley says.

"Maybe," Lo says. "Maybe it's pointless. Maybe it's stupid. Maybe it's actual suicide. But whatever this thing is, I'm not gonna let it stab me in the back. It wants to come for me, it's gonna have to look me in the eye."

When Harley says she can't do it, can't be the part of the plan Lo wants them to be, Lo tells them, "It doesn't matter if you don't know how, kid. Just make some fuckin' noise."

*What does it take to kill a god? The same thing it takes
to create them.*
– From Darrow Foroi's liner notes

THE MUSIC DRIFTS ON the wind throughout what's left of the Questing Beast Renaissance Festival, gliding over the faire-turned-battlefield, its servants bowing, kneeling in its presence.

The only things that remain are corpses.

It is an empty world, but it is also a blank one. One ripe for a reset, a rebirth, to be made great again. Degeneracy washed clean, to be replaced with purity.

But then there's something else.

An electronic squelch.

The world is not empty. Not yet.

The music moves, the chanting and its acolytes following it, hunting that electronic squelch, the voice coming through a loudspeaker, and it finds that horrid *thing* that's playing at being a woman at the rear of the faire, kneeling in the center of the largest stage.

"IT'S HERE."

Lo looks up when Harley says it, and they can almost see it; an absence of something, like a rift in the world pulling in all color and light, all sound and hope. The thing creeps forward down the path towards the main stage towards where what's left of Darrow Foroi stands. Lo doesn't know how they know it's doing it without eyes, but they swear that music, that absence, is looking right at them.

They feel its hate.

Lo lifts the microphone to their lips.

"Come on down," Lo says, their voice booming through the speakers. "Front row center's wide open for you, motherfucker." When they speak, that absence in front of them ripples, and Lo swears they feel its discomfort at their language.

Trailing behind it are the other attackers, somehow less threatening despite their corporeality. The white knight is among them.

"Are you ready?" Lo asks over their shoulder, not into the mic, refusing to take their eyes off the encroaching force. Behind them, Micah and Tijo are still plugging things in, fiddling with dials and knobs. Harley, not knowing what to do, is just waiting until it's her turn.

"Almost," Micah says. "Can you stall?"

"No problem." Lo raises the microphone again, looks right at that absence, that void from which the music is emanating. "We've got a special show tonight." They raise their hand and point at the thing. "One just for you." Again, their voice reverberates through the speakers and that rift in the world shudders. "Don't like that, huh? Don't like the sound of my voice? Big, bad monster, you afraid of a little girl?" They swished their skirt, the words and the gesture a clear taunt.

In response, the music rises, the organ and the chorus slamming into the world. The attackers begin chanting, and Lo feels things pushed into their head. More of those horrible images, the hateful violence inflicted on those who didn't deserve it. It's there, and despite how much the hateful voice hurts, Lo screams into the mic. A random guttural noise that pushes the images—the organ music—away. The encroaching crowd takes several steps back.

"That's it, isn't it?" Lo smirks. "You weren't a fan of that at the motel, were you?"

Over Lo's shoulder, Micah calls, "We're ready!"

Lo smiles. "Well, that was just a taste."

They look over at Harley, who's taken up Evan's position among the drums, at Micah on the guitar, and Tijo at the keyboard. They'll have to do without a bass player. They all give Lo go signals. Lo takes a deep breath and turns back to the absence, to the crowd storming the stage exactly how Lo once feared they might.

But they don't fear these people anymore. They're brave, sure, but they're even angrier. That anger starts in their stomach and it coils as they pull in a breath, winds and curls in their chest, becoming a clenched fist as the aggressors climb the stage, surging forward under the power of the surging choice music.

And then, together, Darrow Foroi lets it rip.

It is not music, but *noise*. Disjointed notes powering outward with the force of a hurricane. Tijo slams experimental notes on the keys as Micah shreds so hard it's like the guitar is going to catch fire, the strings threatening to snap under the force of his strumming. Harley wails on the drum kit like a child on Christmas morning, smashing everything before her, hitting as hard as she can with no regard for the rhythm or even the instruments themselves. Even absent Danny and Evan, it's like when they played together for the first time, letting the feel of the music flow through them, focusing on feeling over technicality.

And as the noise reaches its pitch, Lo lets out their held-in scream. The coiled-up croon in their chest escapes, tearing their throat and ripping past their teeth and blasting into the microphone and out into the world.

What they all make together is only music by the broadest definition. It is random and chaotic and nonsensical. It is a rebellion, a screaming and tearing forth from a womb in which they did not know they resided. For Lo, it is the cracking of a steel-shelled egg that's served as their prison for far too long. With those initial notes the new Darrow Foroi become awful, red things flailing against the world in the only way they know how.

The first wave of attackers who've climbed onto the stage itself are entirely obliterated by the sound wave. The white-armored knight, bereft of his horse, makes it to within a foot of Lo before he's hit by the shape of their scream. Lo keeps singing, keeps screaming, keeps holding the note as the sound wave blasts forward, knocks him off his feet and hauls him into the air. Lo watches as their rebellious noise flays him, tears his armor from his skin, and his skin from his muscle, and his muscle from his bones, and those shatter like toothpicks. Shreds of him fall from the sky, pulpy ribbons and chunks of plate armor. The same happens to the entire front row of attackers. The wave of noise picks them up off the ground and mulches them, not ripping them to bits so much as liquifying them, turning them into torrents of red that rain from the sky.

Unforecasted thunder rips the sky above them apart as the band keeps playing, as Lo looks over their shoulder and yells, "Godkiller!", their album's climax. Once they realize what's happening, Micah and Tijo course-correct. Harley tries her best, keeping up smashing the drums as the beginning of the song dropkicks the next wave of attackers as they attempt to climb the stage. Thunder slams again, without lightning, and it starts to rain, the steady *shhhh* of droplets coming down all around them. But it isn't water.

It's blood.

Lo looks through the crimson rain to the rippling, shimmering attackers, and among them they see Evan and Danny. Unlike the other attackers, they're not advancing, but it doesn't look like it'll be for long. They stand there like they're pained, like they're struggling to stay still, and Lo knows the invisible force is working its will on them.

Do it, those looks tell them. *Do what we came here to do.*

Lo nods.

They draw in a breath, not for another mindless scream, but the beginning of the song. Micah wrings the guitar's neck. Tijo cracks keys. Harley punches holes in the drums, chips the sticks against the cymbals, splinters flying. Rained blood sprays from each and every one of them as they work their instruments. Darrow Foroi plays longer. They play harder. They scream with the taste of blood in their mouths, shred with slick fingertips, slam with wet drumsticks.

The organ music picks up, the chanting rises, and together they form a rival wave, musical currents smashing against one another above and through the crowd, evaporating those friendlies unlucky enough to be struck. The rival notes play higher, louder, entangling and fighting in the air above the band and the attackers, manifested as swirls of audible color and splashes of visible sound. Lightning crackles and smoke pours forth, invisible colors and spectrums tearing their way into the world through this elemental clashing. The air before them sears and burns, gouts of fire and eruptions of lava spewing forth from rends in reality itself as two enormous figures manifest above the crowd.

On the side of the absence, the attacking crowd, there is an enormous, white knight, covered head-to-toe in plated armor and wielding a massive, white sword, staring down through the sky, the smoke, the rain of blood, at Darrow Foroi.

But rising up to protect them is another shape, one just as large as the knight, a lithe, red figure in little more than leather armor, a spear in both hands. They can't see much else, its back to them.

At first, the show looks like a smoke projection, images pushed out onto dry ice Darrow Foroi has seen at dozens of concerts before. Except there is a reality to them here, a wholeness that almost makes the band stop, makes their notes hiccup until Harley smashes the drums again, drawing them back to the fight. They scream, they keep playing, keep obliterating wave after wave of attackers as they try to climb the stage.

Above them, through the rain of blood, they see the two enormous shapes clash, see the red figure knock the knight's sword away. It's much faster in its leather armor, and crawls spiderlike around the knight's back, up its shoulders, grabbing its faceplate to wrench it open, which is when Lo and everyone else sees the figure's face; a skinless, eyeless skull, devilish horns sprouting from its forehead. The shape cracks the knight's faceplate open like a turtle's shell, and there's not enough time to see what the knight looks like as the climax of "Godkiller" kicks in and the skeleton regurgitates, spewing a hot waterfall of fire and lava over the knight's face, into its suit, the fire finding its way out through chinks and joints in the armor, boiling the plates.

The final wave of attackers are blasted into nothingness by errant waves of visible music, among them Danny and Evan. Lo glimpses them one final time before the force of their notes overpowers the organ music, the wave annihilating the entire crowd, atomizing them, adding them to the rain of blood that pours down upon the band. Watching the enormous, impossible shapes above them, they keep going; Lo draws breath; Micah raises his pick high above his head; Tijo cracks his knuckles; Harley holds the drumsticks aloft. And with their final musical crash, the fire burns the knight and the organ music and the ethereal choir out of the world.

When the Dawn Queen perishes, the sky itself is set aflame. Embers of her corpse burn holes into the universe, revealing new, frightening, beautiful possibilities.

– From Darrow Foroi's liner notes

Darrow Foroi collapses onstage, all of them looking out into the stands where the crowd once was, the rain of blood falling from the sky slowing to a trickle.

After a moment of silence, Lo looks over their shoulder. Micah and Tijo nod at them, and then they look at Harley. "You okay, kid?"

Covered in blood, hair matted to her scalp, red in her teeth, Harley smiles.

Laughs. Her laughter becomes sobs and then laughter again. And one by one, everyone else follows.

The police arrive to The Questing Beast Renaissance Festival. Late, as always. Hundreds of nonsensical 911 calls led to the mobilization of squad cars and SWAT vans, helicopters and even anti-riot tanks (this is America, after all). The modern-day army storms the medieval fairgrounds, but the action is over. All they find are shredded corpses and a few dozen scattered groups of survivors, all spouting what sounds like gibberish about monsters.

THE INCIDENT BECOMES KNOWN as the Questing Beast Festival Massacre.

There are rumors about local white supremacist groups, such as the Brotherhood of the Black Cross, the Cyklops, the Church of the Pyramidia, especially due to the very obvious pattern with the dead and injured. It is a theory no one in any position of power will acknowledge, even though those attacked and killed are all minorities, women, people from the LGBT+ community.

Spokespersons from a dozen different law enforcement departments dispute this claim. They talk on and on about finding the truth, about taking time to grieve, about making sure justice prevails and not jumping to conclusions, their words nothing but endless roundabouts, as they always are after such mass tragedies. The president refers to the events as a tragedy, says that because the local police are dumbfounded, the Bureau of Special Services will be handling the case. They will bring those responsible to justice.

But after a couple weeks the press conferences and the op-eds and the photo ops and the donation drives stop. Everyone seems ready to move on to the next tragedy, a pretty, young white girl who suffers an attempted kidnapping from her own porch by an unidentified assailant. And even before that tragedy is fully digested, there is another. And another. And soon, the Questing Beast Festival Massacre is largely forgotten.

No one is ever found responsible.

No one is ever arrested.

But there are whispers.

HARLEY RETURNS TO HER house only once after the Questing Beast ordeal. To pack up things for her move. She's eighteen, is legally responsible for herself, but her aunt in Baltimore told her she'd be more than happy to have Harley come and live with her, at least until college starts in a couple months. Holstenwall College is close. She'll still be able to visit.

Harley looks through the windshield of Darrow Foroi's rented van as they cross the state line from Florida into Georgia. She'll be back one day, she thinks. This goodbye isn't forever. Just for now. Now it's not quite safe.

But one day it will be.

Darrow Foroi is a place. At least, that's the in-world explanation. But, now, elsewhere, somewhere far away from Alor, it is also a group. It exists in multiple places, just as the legend of Darrow Foroi, of the Questing Beast Festival Massacre, works its way into rock lore. Because everything was off the record, under the table, there is nothing official tying them to the renaissance faire. They are never even questioned, just quick, scratchy statements as EMTs patched them up.

The account Nathan Biggs gives to the police of the incident is of an unknown-to-him white supremacist group.

The tale he tells to his daughter, and eventually to his granddaughter in a watered-down version, is quite different. It's the story of a band of heroes, and their leader, a princess. Heroes who fought against the forces of evil. Heroes who took a loss, who didn't save everyone, but who fought. And that's the point, isn't it? To fight, even if you think you might lose.

The story changes with the telling, as all stories do, so that all versions are true, in a way, because all versions exist at once. But no matter the version, no matter its alterations or variables, there is always one constant—the heroes standing up before the villains.

Darrow Foroi's second album, *The Magnitude of Story*, is about this, about what a story is, what a legend is. About how it changes, about what versions are true for you. It is still about Alor, still about something more than just escapism, because that isn't who they are, Lo thinks, stepping out onto the stage in a dress and combat boots. Darrow Foroi, to its members, isn't just a band anymore. It isn't just therapy, a way for them to channel their feelings about the world around them. They'd committed to something long-term, something eternal, the moment they agreed to the Questing Beast show, whether they knew it or not. It's something more now. *They* are something more. They had to be, ever since they burned that terrible white knight out of the sky. Because there are plenty more of them out there. On school boards and city council chambers and police chief offices. All the way up to the White House.

That's why, as Lo takes to the mic at the beginning of their first official show in Florida, their first show in the year 2025, they make their first set a tribute to the police officer at the front door of the club, calling him out. The cop who's trying to make it to the front of the stage to make an arrest, because what he's seeing—this band in dresses—is a clear violation of public decency and he cannot let this deviancy continue.

But he has no hope of getting past the surging crowd.

THE END

Acknowledgements

There are a ton of people to thank for bringing this book to life. First, obviously, there's David-Jack and Slashic Horror Press for taking a chance on "rock band vs. sentient neofascist music at a renaissance festival," which is perhaps my wildest pitch ever.

To Steve Neal and djp for talking me off a ledge with the initial draft of this book when I wanted to completely rewrite it. Thanks to Zack Marsh for helping bring the faire to life and making it metal as hell. Another huge shoutout to Will and Kristen of Guide to the Unknown, for giving me the idea to give a few things the Alex Casey treatment, and to everyone who was there for Regicide, *this* is the kind of unhinged I wanted to be.

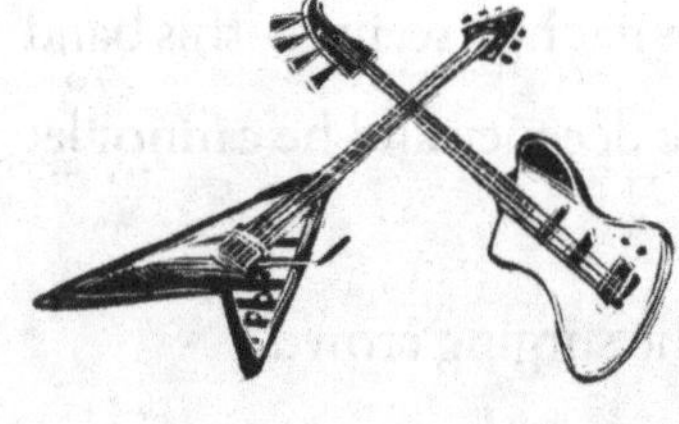

I also have to throw up devil horns to many of the musicians that provided the soundtrack for the many, *many* hours I spent working on this novella; Sleep Token, Halestorm, 10 Years, Linkin Park, Lacuna Coil, Tenacious D, Bear McCreary, Coheed and Cambria, Ursine Vulpine, and Junkie XL, just to name a few.

And obviously thank *you*, reader, for picking this book up. Hopefully it helps inspire you to get behind the mic, in whatever way that might be for you.

Rock on.

About the Author

TT Madden (they/them) is a Pushcart-nominated, genderfluid, mixed-race writer who refuses to keep "politics" out of their writing (if you couldn't already tell from the book about fighting against sentient neofascist music). They've written in the sandboxes of big IPs, helping create the *Blair Witch* and *Agatha Christie* tabletop mystery games for Hunt a Killer, but they much prefer writing smaller, weirder stories that make you uncomfortable, but in a way you hopefully want to explore more.

Their short prose has been published by Ghoulish Tales, Bag of Bones Press, and Speculation Publications, among others. Their novellas have been published by Off Limits Press, Neon Hemlock, Little Ghost Books, and Timber Ghost Press, with many more forthcoming.

They can be found at ttmaddenwrites.carrd.co when they're not wandering the woods around their home, looking for spooky inspiration.

www.ingramcontent.com/pod-product-compliance
Lightning Source LLC
Chambersburg PA
CBHW010342170726
48283CB00009B/2927